# The Revenge Pact

## A Madly Bad at Love Novel

### Brooke Stanton

Coco & Bee

**The Revenge Pact** by Brooke Stanton
Copyright © 2023 by Brooke Stanton. All rights reserved.

*To all the smut lovers out there.*
*This book is for you.*

# Chapter 1

## *Eva*

"I fucked Joe last night."

The words drifted out of the bridal suite, slammed into my chest, and dropped like a stone into my gut.

"Shut up, Ashley," came a second voice, lower, with a razor-sharp edge. Rachel Hoffman. My college roommate and bestie.

I froze in the hotel corridor, too stunned to move. Ashley's confession gripped me like a vise I couldn't wrench myself out of.

"If you ruin this day for Eva because you're jealous, I'll Samson and Delilah your hair." Rachel's voice dripped with the threat. "I'm not fucking kidding, Ash."

A sharp cramp pulled at the arch in my right foot, but I didn't dare move for fear they'd hear the rustle of my ridiculously large Cinderella wedding dress, and I absolutely had to know if Ashley was telling the truth because:

1. I was walking down the aisle in twenty minutes with the aforementioned Joe.

2. Ashley was Joe's ex-girlfriend.

3. This wedding had to happen.

"Why would I be jealous?" Ashley purred. "I've been fucking Joe for the past three months. He said Eva hasn't spread her legs since they got engaged."

I gasped, and my hand flew to my mouth to cover the noise. Prickly heat spread over my bare shoulders, and I sucked down a tunnel of air, trying to clear the fog this bomb had exploded in my head.

Ashley and I had always tolerated each other, but we'd never been close. Rachel and she had grown up together and they both went to Syracuse University, where I'd been freshman roommates with Rachel. Rachel and I were instant besties, and since Ashley was already part of the group, we had no choice but to be friends.

When I met Joe, Ashley was dating some hotshot hockey player. I didn't know Ashley and Joe had dated until later, but she said she didn't care.

Obviously, she was a lying bitch.

Rachel kicked the bathroom door shut with her heel, and I flattened myself against the wall next to it, unseen.

*Shitballs.*

I pressed my ear against the door, but I couldn't

hear a damn thing. There was an inch crack at the bottom, and I got down on my belly, my skirt billowing around me. I strained to listen, but all I heard were murmurs of voices.

Rachel would be freaking out, trying to figure out how to shut Ashley down and save the day for me. Rachel and Ashley may have known each other longer, but Rachel was fiercely loyal to me (and I was to her).

My heart thundered behind the boning underneath the lace overlay of my dress. I glared at the closed door, debating what to do. I wanted to rip Ashley's stupid black hair out of her stupid scalp.

The voices grew closer, and the doorknob turned. I scurried to the room across the hall and ducked inside, keeping the door open a crack.

"Not a word," Rachel hissed, their dresses crinkling as they walked away. "Say it."

"Fine," Ashley grumbled, and then they were gone.

I shoved my billowing skirt through the doorway and crashed into the bridal suite. I circled the room, distress and confusion accosting all my senses, making it impossible to think clearly.

Moments ago I'd been in there getting ready with Rachel and my mom, laughing and joking, oblivious to the wreckage ahead.

The guests were outside on the great lawn, taking their places for the ceremony. Obviously, I should call off the wedding, except I couldn't, because Joe and I did something really stupid.

We eloped five months ago.

I was from Toronto and it had been my idea to get hitched early so I could start the application process for my citizenship before my green card expired.

It hadn't made sense to let the green card lapse when we were so close to getting married. That's why we went to city hall right after New Year's Eve.

No biggie.

Except now it was a colossal biggie. If I walked out on this marriage right now, it could screw everything up. I was in a kind of limbo, waiting for the interview to prove our marriage was legit. Only after that would my U.S. citizenship be permanent and secure. Without it I could lose my job, my life, everything I'd worked for up until this moment of my life.

*Fuck.*

*Fuckity fuck fuck fucking balls.*

I tore at the buttons at the back of my bodice, but I couldn't undo them. The corset was too tight. My air was constricted, and starbursts flashed in front of my eyes.

I screamed in frustration, yanking with all my might. But the damn dress wouldn't budge.

"Evelyn?" a deep voice said behind me.

My spine went ramrod straight, and I sucked in a sharp breath.

Ethan Steele stepped into the room, and as he did, the walls closed in around me.

He wore a morning suit and top hat, like some

duke in a Regency drama. His dark eyebrows furrowed at the sight of me.

Air. I needed air.

My fingers clawed at the fabric, ripping it, but no air would come. My knees buckled, and Ethan leaned forward, catching me in his arms right before I hit the floor.

I wiggled in his grasp, hating him a little more than usual.

"Stop fighting me." He gripped my shoulders and twisted me around, trying to guide me and my ginormous skirt over to the small settee.

"Let go." I yanked out of his grip and fell face-first onto the cushions of the sofa, my hoop skirt lifting up and over my ass.

"You okay down there?" Ethan asked above me, a smirk in his voice.

I wore a lace thong, and I was flashing him my tanned ass, but I didn't care. He could look all he wanted. It was the least of my worries.

And it was a really good ass.

I shimmied to the ground and flipped over, lying on the floor and glaring at him, but then the whole not-being-able-to-breathe thing started again and I gripped my sides. His frown dropped, and he sank to his knees, pulling me up to a sitting position.

"What's wrong, Evelyn?"

"Stop acting"—gasp—"like you care"—gasp—"and help me"—gasp—"out of this." A dizzy spell overtook me, and I slumped sideways.

"Please," I whispered, the last scraps of my dignity floating away. I needed help, and I didn't care who gave it to me.

Even the most despised man in my life.

# Chapter 2

## *Eva*

I kneeled on the carpet, vulnerable and desperate. Two things I never wanted to be in front of the man who had tried to stop this wedding the moment Joe and I got engaged.

Ethan's left arm circled my waist, and he yanked my back to his chest, settling my ass on his firm thighs. I bent forward, panting into the plush carpet.

The sounds of the pre-wedding classical music seeped into the room, and I squirmed, needing to get out of this dress so I could breathe but also needing to get to the ceremony.

"Keep still, dammit." Ethan gripped me tighter, trying to tame me. His right hand slid up my back and popped open the line of buttons down the bodice, releasing my ribs from their cage.

He threw the top aside, and the brisk air wrapped around my bare abdomen and lace-clad breasts, cooling me instantly. I fell forward, swallowing large gulps of air.

Ethan hovered close by, his arms crossed, his face stern. "What the fuck, Evelyn? Are you having cold feet?"

"No! I..." My chin wobbled, and I clamped my jaw shut.

I could do this. I could wipe the black streaks of mascara off my face, put my top back on, and get through today. If I didn't go out there and act the part of the happy bride, it could majorly screw up my life.

My application could be put into the deny pile if someone found out I'd called off my wedding, despite being technically married. You can't hide shit these days.

Nope. No way. I would not let Asswipe Ashley ruin my life. At least, not in public.

"Help me put this cage back on." I snatched the corset top to my nearly naked chest.

If Joe was a cheating scumbag, I'd deal with it. I solved problems every day of my life. It's what I was good at. It gave me comfort.

I'd find a way out. Just not right now.

I knelt before Ethan. His chestnut hair was disheveled from the effort of manhandling me, and he shoved his hands through it, arranging the pieces back in place.

My hoop skirt swallowed me up, which was good since the lace, strapless bra was nearly see-through.

Ethan had been averting his eyes ever since he'd torn the bodice from my chest.

"What's this about?" Ethan asked, but the edge in his voice had softened. His hands were warm and sure as he wrapped the corset around my ribs.

"Wedding day jitters." I held it in place, and Ethan slid the buttons through the delicate satin hoops.

"Bullshit," he said.

I tensed, ignoring the soft touch of his finger pads as he dressed me.

"Why would I confide in you?" I asked. "You hate me. Anything I say you'll run off and tell Joe. All I'm asking for is a moment of compassion. And to shut up about what you saw in here."

Ethan silently continued buttoning. When he was done, he sat back on his heels.

"I don't hate you, Evelyn," he said.

"Despise. Hate. Loathe. Does it matter the verbiage?" I shoved my heeled feet to standing and crossed my arms. "By the way, the feeling is mutual."

"You've made that clear on more than one occasion," he deadpanned.

I waved my hands back and forth, clearing the air between us. "Let's forget all that right now."

I swept to the door, Ethan jumping aside to make room for my excessive skirt. My hands gripped the doorjamb, a dizzy spell slamming into me.

"I can't do it," I whimpered. My breathing shallowed again, the fabric strangling my lungs.

Ethan placed firm hands on my upper arms and

9

held tight to me. I didn't even care that he saw the tears pricking my eyes.

How was I going to look at Joe and fake it through this?

"Can we have a truce? For five minutes," Ethan said, his bright blue eyes penetrating mine. "Pretend I'm someone else. You won't make it through the ceremony if you don't release what's upsetting you. You're a mess."

Tears plopped onto my cheeks.

"What happened?" he asked gently. His kindness was more unnerving than his usual indifference toward me.

I dabbed at my face with the heel of my palm. Ethan slid his lavender pocket square out of his formal jacket and handed it to me. I gently soaked up my tears. Crying helped, and I was breathing deeply again.

"It's Ashley. I overheard her. I..." Tears fell again. "She said she and Joe are..."

I couldn't say it. Not to Ethan. It was too humiliating.

"Sleeping together," Ethan finished.

"You knew!" Fury flared in my veins, and I shot my hands out, striking him in his chest. It was like hitting a brick wall. I shook my hands out and then struck him again, but this time he was ready and caught my wrists.

I tried to strike him, but he tightened his hold, and I winced.

"Stop that," he said, his voice low. I pulled back but

he yanked my wrists, and I slammed into his chest, our hearts vibrating against each other's ribs.

Ethan's eyes caught mine and we froze, lost in this weird tornado of anger and something else that was strange and completely unexpected.

He released me as if I'd scalded him, and I stumbled backward.

"You knew he was fucking her?" I hissed, steadying myself against the wall.

His jaw ground under his skin. "I suspected. But I didn't know for sure."

"Yeah, right," I scoffed.

"If I'd known, I would've told you," he grumbled, his gaze searing hot.

"Ha!" I barked. "I'm sure you would've run to me with the news."

It sounded sarcastic, but I meant it. If Ethan had a reason that would stop the wedding, he would've used it. He never wanted me to marry his oldest friend. I'd overheard him say it to Joe right after the engagement. *Asking her to marry you is the stupidest thing you've ever done. And you've done some stupid things.*

And then they'd laughed like it was a big joke.

Now, we glared at each other, but then he ran his hand down his face and exhaled loudly, the tension releasing from his muscles.

"What do you need?" he asked calmly. "Do you want me to get Rachel? She'd be the best person to tell everyone the wedding is off."

"The wedding isn't off." I shoved several loose

11

pieces of my honey-blonde hair back into my updo, regaining my composure.

"Why would you marry him now?" Ethan looked at me with disdain. "He's cheating on you. Have some self-worth."

"I have worth, asshole, but there's no point making a scene." I cut him with a sharp scowl. "We're already married."

The color drained from Ethan's olive skin. "What are you talking about?"

"We went to city hall a few months ago. Because of the green card issue." I walked to the mirror and wiped the river of mascara from my cheeks.

"But—"

"Drop it, Ethan," I said. "This won't get fixed by stopping the ceremony. It'll just cause a lot of unnecessary drama. The deed's been done."

Ethan's look of shock turned to something darker—pity, sorrow, disgust—I didn't know, but I'd rather him loathe me than pity me.

"You were wrong, by the way." I stepped toward him, my fingernail poking into his chest. "Getting engaged to me wasn't the stupidest thing Joe has ever done."

The look of shock on Ethan's face was totally worth the reveal. He had no idea that I'd heard him all those months ago when he'd shit all over my new engagement.

"I may not be able to get out of this dumpster fire

today," I said, Ethan's heart thundering in his chest under my finger.

I cocked the side of my mouth up, delighted I was getting to him.

"But he's gonna pay for this. You both are."

# Chapter 3

## *Ethan*

Eva was right. I never wanted her to marry Joe. I had no idea why he fell so goddamn hard for her. She was boring and predictable. Since she'd met Joe, she'd planned and organized their lives into tidy boxes.

Tonight had been the first time I'd seen a hair out of place. Her meltdown was like watching a natural disaster. I was horrified and fascinated all at once.

Across the ballroom, Joe was dancing with the few remaining wedding guests to a disco song, while I sat at one of the empty round tables. It was past midnight, and most of the guests had retired.

Eva barely made it through the ceremony. Tears ran down her cheeks the entire time. A few guests commented that it was strange to see her so emotional. She usually held her cards close to her chest, not revealing what was behind that perfect facade.

After the speeches, she'd disappeared. Some story

about bad fish. Obviously, it was an excuse to hide for the rest of the night.

She always had a contingency plan in place if things took an unexpected turn, but Joe fucking his ex-girlfriend was obviously not something she'd considered on her list of things that could go awry on her wedding day.

Joe collapsed in a chair next to one of his work friends, laughing and chugging his beer.

If my new wife had food poisoning, I'd be with her, not closing down the party. He hadn't checked on her once.

"Scoot." Rachel, Eva's maid of honor, pulled the seat out next to me.

She was clad in her black lace bridesmaid dress and her pastel-pink hair had fallen out of her topknot and lay in a curly mess around her shoulders.

I liked Rachel. She was a bit off-the-wall, but you always knew where you stood with her.

"I thought you left hours ago," I said.

Rachel adjusted the pink bra strap that had fallen down her shoulder and tucked her bare foot under her thigh.

"I was with Eva in the room. She's a wreck, so I gave her a Valium and now she's sleeping."

"Because of the food poisoning?" I asked, feigning ignorance.

"No, you idiot. Because Joe is banging Ashley."

I choked on my sip of scotch.

"I know you helped her earlier," Rachel said,

crossing her arms and eyeing me suspiciously. "I'm surprised you didn't leave her there and go high-five your boy."

"Fuck him." I ground my teeth together.

Rachel widened her eyes, surprised at my response.

"So you *did* know he was cheating."

"No." I glowered. "But I've learned a few things about *my boy* recently. So I wasn't surprised."

Rachel turned fully toward me. "What the hell are you talking about?"

*Shit.* Why had I said that?

"Nothing," I grumbled into my drink.

"Oh, hell no. You don't get to drop that grenade and then shut down. You owe it to Eva to confess if you knew something about Joe. You shit on her from the moment you met her, and guess what? It's Joe who turned out to be the asshole."

I glared at the stained, white tablecloth.

Joe met Eva during my last year at Syracuse University, but I was already living in Manhattan. I'd been hired at a small financial company to help design their new app and was finishing up my degree online at night while I worked during the day.

Joe had graduated from his trade school two years prior and was working for a contractor in Syracuse, managing a new build, when he met Eva.

She was also a senior at Syracuse, but I'd never met her until I came up one weekend to visit Joe.

I joined them at a house party, and everyone was

laughing and drinking but Eva, who sat in a corner working on her resume.

That wasn't a big deal, but Joe is an affectionate and big-hearted guy, and Eva barely acknowledged him all night.

The entire weekend Joe padded around her like a puppy dog, eager for any attention she threw at him, but she was cold and aloof.

Everything had to be her way, and I was shocked that Joe went along. She'd planned out their entire future after one month. It was unnerving.

Women were usually all over Joe. He worked out like it was his job, and there was something about the rugged-construction-worker thing that made women go wild.

Eva didn't seem to care about any of that, and I wondered why she was with him at all.

I understood why Joe was with her.

It was ironic, but her indifference was intoxicating to Joe. He came across as self-assured and confident, but his ego was fragile, and Eva would've been a challenge. I doubt he realized this on a conscious level. But Joe definitely fit the mold of someone wanting what they couldn't have.

A year later, when Joe asked her to marry him, I couldn't take it. The last thing I wanted for my best friend was to wake up one day and realize he was in a loveless marriage.

My parents had barely tolerated each other, only staying together for my sister and me. But their bitterness seeped into everything, and we had a miserable childhood. It drove my father to drink and my mother into a deep depression.

I wanted Joe to be with a woman who saw how goddamn amazing he was.

But I'd been wrong.

Joe wasn't amazing. He was a piece of shit.

"Eva's not the only one Joe betrayed," I said, the words burning my throat.

A shadow fell over Rachel's pierced brow. "What are you talking about?"

If I was going down this road, I had to spit it out fast. "Joe slept with Jasmin."

Rachel gasped. "While you were together?"

"A few weeks after we broke up."

"Damn." Rachel clucked.

Jasmin was my college girlfriend and the first girl I'd loved. When she dumped me, I was a wreck.

"While I lay on his couch, wallowing in my misery, he was fucking her behind my back." I clamped my mouth closed, bile rising up my esophagus.

"And you stayed friends with him?" Rachel asked. I cut my gaze toward her, and she threw her hands up. "I'm not judging, just asking."

"I only found out a few weeks ago. I didn't want to ruin the wedding." I flagged down a waiter and asked for water. I'd already said too much. "Not for Joe's sake. But for Eva's. I'm not her biggest fan, but I'm not a complete dick. Joe hadn't betrayed *her*. Well...not that I'd known about."

Rachel glanced over my shoulder at Joe gyrating his hips on the dance floor to a Bee Gees song, his thick shoulders transparent through his sweaty dress shirt.

"What are you going to do?" Rachel asked, steepling her fingers under her chin.

I gulped my water. "If I confront him now, it might mess things up for Eva, right?"

Rachel nodded and tapped her pointed nail on the side of her champagne glass, thinking.

"Eva can't divorce Joe yet, and when the shock wears off, she's gonna feel trapped," Rachel said. "She's not one to sit back and let life happen. She'll want retaliation."

"Ha," I said without humor. "She's not the type to get revenge. It's too messy."

"You'd be surprised," Rachel said. She didn't give a further explanation, and I didn't push it.

I stood up and punched my arms into the sleeves of my jacket and shoved my ridiculous top hat on my head. I had to get out of there.

"If she wants to fuck with him, let me know," I said, a sneer on my lips. "I'm in."

# Chapter 4

## *Eva*

Rachel slid her phone across the bar until it rested in front of me. There was an article on the screen entitled "Ten Ways to Get Revenge on a Cheater."

"If I wanted to blow up my life, I would've done it at the wedding." I sighed.

I sipped my beer, then raised it to a colleague who was waving at me across the lounge. We were at a speakeasy in the West Village, which we entered through a secret bookcase at the back of a dive bar.

I'd never heard of this place, but my boss organized the happy hour after we signed a popular sex education podcast to our label at Dreamary, the media company where I worked as a junior producer.

"Half my colleagues are here." I clicked the side button, and Rachel's screen went black. "This is so not the time or place."

Rachel lifted her phone, unperturbed, and turned it back on.

"One," she read. "Spray-paint their car or other property with CHEATER or LIAR."

She glanced at me, and we both shook our heads. Joe didn't own a car, and it would be too public. We needed to be stealth.

"Two, put Nair in the offender's shampoo."

Again, not gonna happen because Joe had recently shaved his head.

"He has hair on other parts of his body." Rachel smiled over her Kir Royale. "Do you think Ashely likes the bald seal look?"

I laughed, but the anchor attached to my despair sank into my gut, and I sucked down a shaky breath.

The wedding was two weeks ago, and I'd grinned through it, breaking down several times. Luckily, the wedding guests and my family thought I was overcome with joy.

Only Rachel knew the truth.

And Ethan.

Rachel had snatched me away moments before the ceremony to tell me what Ashley had confessed, but before she opened her mouth, I told her I'd overheard them in the bathroom, then I quickly explained that I had to go through with the ceremony.

Rachel knew Joe and I were already married, so this wasn't a shocker.

I'd left halfway through the reception, and Rachel's

lie that I had food poisoning also got me out of sex on my wedding night.

"This sucks," I said into my hands, my chin wobbling.

I could not cry at a work function. Too many hours had already been spent sobbing in the office bathroom.

The week post-wedding had been surreal. It felt like I was an interloper in someone else's life. There were moments in the day when it would hit me unexpectedly, and I'd dash off to the bathroom and cry.

"I had a plan, goddammit," I said furiously, strangling the neck of my beer bottle.

"I know." Rachel rubbed my back.

This was a reversal from last year when she'd been the one crying on my shoulder after she'd found her birth mother. It had not been the Hallmark reunion she'd imagined.

I took several deep breaths and shoved the burning grief into the box I kept it in most of the day. I thanked the Goddess above that Joe was working on a new building project an hour upstate and I didn't have to plaster on a fake persona around him, but at night I'd sob myself to sleep.

We'd delayed our honeymoon until the fall when Joe's work slowed down and I could use the PTO from my job. Otherwise, I may have strangled him in his sleep with my wedding lingerie.

"I made a vision board. I had action steps. I'd filled all my quarter-life goals." Overwhelmed by my unknown future, my voice broke.

Rachel rested her chin on my shoulder. "I know, honey."

I began listing them, seeing the large whiteboard that sat on my nightstand in my head. "Graduate college with honors. Check. Meet my forever man. Check. Get a job at a socially responsible company with a good salary and benefits. Check. Get married before twenty-five. Check. Have two babies. Retire at sixty, travel the world, and live happily ever after!"

A few heads turned at my explosion.

Rachel pulled her bottom jaw sideways in mock distress. "I think you've moved past denial and into rage," she quipped.

"I can't do this right now." I waved my hands in the air, clearing away the anxiety which threatened to suffocate me. "I can't do this now."

I scratched my neck, the skin hot and itchy.

"Did you find out any more info about the interview?" Rachel asked, clicking her glittery claw-like nails together. I tried nails like those once, but I almost poked my eye out putting my contacts in, so I opted for short, blunt nails.

Too bad. They could've been useful against Joe.

"I got nowhere when I called the immigration office. Bureaucracy at its finest. I couldn't get ahold of a real person. The site says it can take months to a year for the citizenship application to be finalized. But when I read a subreddit with people who'd gone through it, they said it ranged from two months to nine." I dropped my forehead to the sticky bar. "I can't wait that long."

Rachel reached out to comfort me, but I batted her hand away.

Enough.

"If you can't change it, change how you view it," I parroted one of my favorite quotes. "Entertain me with those revenge ideas."

Rachel smiled, delighted, and continued reading the article. "Three. Sell all his clothes."

She put the phone between us, and we took turns reading them aloud.

"Get a revenge bod," I read and rolled my eyes. "I just whipped these curves into wedding shape. I've never felt better. Next."

"Delete work files," Rachel read.

I raised my eyebrows. That could be a possibility.

"Share their infidelity on social media," I continued. "No. At least, not yet."

A twenty-something woman with strawberry-blonde hair slid through the crowd next to me and ordered a drink.

"Replace phone numbers in his phone," Rachel said.

"Maybe." I chewed on my bottom lip and scrolled up. "Hide frozen fish in his suitcase before a trip."

"I'm intrigued." A young woman leaning against the bar nearby turned to me and smiled, a sparkling rosé in her delicate fingers. She was petite, her skin pale with light freckling on her arms. Her eyelids pinched together when she grinned, her eyes almost disappearing. "I hope you don't mind me butting in. I'm Alexis."

"As in Sex with Lex?" I asked, recognizing her. She was the host of the new podcast we'd acquired.

"The one and only." She raised her flute glass, and we clinked glasses.

"I love your show." Rachel beamed. "I'm all about anything sex-positive."

"You're a therapist, right?" I asked, turning my barstool so I faced her, creating a semicircle.

"I have a master's in clinical psychology and my doctorate in human sexuality. I've always been fascinated by how our culture has dealt with, or rather, not dealt with sex. So I combined my two passions." Alexis wiggled her eyebrows. "And I feel like I walked in on a very interesting conversation."

"We were debating how to get revenge on a cheater," Rachel said.

"Oh shit." Alexis slapped her hand over her mouth. "Did someone cheat on one of you?"

"That would be me," Rachel quipped, covering for me.

I obviously couldn't let Alexis know the truth. The circle was already two people too wide with Rachel and Ethan knowing. Oh, and the perpetrators, Joe and Ashley.

"I want to nail this guy," Rachel said, a bite in her voice.

"What have you come up with so far?" Alexis asked.

"Destroying prized property. Messing with his phone. That kind of thing."

"Be careful with the property stuff. You could land in jail." Alexis shrugged apologetically. "Not to be a downer. But I've seen it happen. What else?"

Rachel took the phone and read the entire list out loud.

"What's the most popular type of revenge that you've heard?" I asked Alexis, leaning forward.

"For women, the number one tactic is a revenge affair," Alexis said.

Rachel's face lit up, but I frowned.

"That seems like a lot of work," I said. "And fighting fire with fire."

"It wouldn't really be an affair," Rachel said for my benefit. "The relationship's over. I'm done with that asswipe, right?"

"I guess. I mean, yes," I said, still pretending Rachel was the one wronged.

My marriage was a sham at this point. We had to stay together for me to secure my citizenship, but the moment I was approved, I was leaving Joe. If I had an affair with someone else, I'd feel zero guilt. But who the hell would I have an affair with?

"I doubt Jo—I mean, Rachel's boyfriend would even care if she had an affair. He's screwing someone else," I said, the ache burrowing into me.

"Men's egos are way more fragile than women's

when it comes to sexual matters," Alexis said. "But if you want to hurt him—and this is Alexis talking, not Lex the therapist—an affair with one of his good friends will cut him deepest. A best friend. Or brother. Or his boss. You know, something that would wreck his ego." Alexis put her hands up. "Not that I'm recommending this. It never ends well. It usually backfires. The woman is emotionally scarred by it, or the boyfriend doesn't care. Or if he does care, it could get violent. Property destroyed, stuff like that."

"It'd be like killing two birds with one stone," Rachel said, typing rapidly on her phone. "The affair could also be a rebound while getting back at the asshole."

Bringing another guy into this was not part of my plan. Not that I had a plan. Not yet. But I'm pretty sure if I did, this would not be it.

"It's too complicated," I said. "First, we'd have to find a friend or boss or whatever. And this friend would have to be up for the affair."

"I have a guy in mind." Rachel smiled cryptically.

I frowned, wondering whom she meant or if she was just saying it for Alexis's sake.

Alexis playfully stuck her fingers in her ears. "I'm not hearing this."

Derrick, my boss, waved Alexis over to where he was chatting with the executive team and she put her finger up, indicating she'd be there in a minute.

"I'll leave you with one more bit of advice," she said, taking the last sip of her drink. "If you do this, there's no coming back. Men are not as forgiving as women."

Alexis slid her empty glass onto the bar and walked away.

"If Joe's pissed enough never to forgive you," Rachel said, dismissing the warning, "then we've won."

"Won what?" a deep voice asked.

I spun around and gaped at Ethan, scraping my gaze down his lean frame. He wore dark jeans and a light pink, short-sleeved, button-down shirt with palm trees all over it.

"Eva is going to—"

I slapped a hand over Rachel's mouth, shutting her up.

"Nothing. Go away." I waved my hand dismissively, but my heart raced.

I was fucked. If Ethan heard any part of our conversation, he'd run and tell Joe. I don't care how nice he was to me on my wedding day.

He crossed his arms, a smug smile on his lips.

"I'm not going anywhere."

# Chapter 5

## *Ethan*

I hadn't seen Eva since the wedding, and the look on her face suggested she wanted to keep it that way. I'd never been outwardly unkind to Eva. Dismissive, sure, but never mean.

While Eva and Joe dated, she was civil to me, but after they got engaged, she treated me like a pariah.

I'd been perplexed by her icy change, but now I knew why. She'd overheard me tell Joe not to marry her.

"What are you doing here?" she asked, pulling a sip from her beer and wiping her lips with the back of her hand.

"Rachel invited me." I smiled.

Eva punched Rachel in the thigh. "Traitor."

"Ethan's the perfect person to help plan your revenge." Rachel bounced on her toes.

"Rachel!" she scoffed. "Have you gone mental?"

"I know you guys hate each other but—" Rachel said.

"I don't hate her," I cut in. Eva could be tedious and dull, but I'd never hated her.

"I absolutely hate him." Eva angled her back to me. There was a little tattoo of a Japanese character on her right shoulder, and I quickly lifted my phone and snapped a picture.

"You can't ostrich me out of existence." I chuckled, enjoying this more than I thought I would. It had been weeks since I'd laughed.

After I found out about Joe and my ex, Jasmin, I'd gone into a dark hole. I teetered between depression and anger. When the anger overwhelmed me, I'd pound the pavement, running more than I had in years, but the depression was harder to tackle.

Exercise helped, but after I showered and the quietness of my apartment surrounded me, my mind would wander to the betrayal.

Joe had been MIA leading up to the wedding. The only contact we had was when I planned his bachelor party, which had been a clichéd event in Atlantic City with gambling and strippers and a steak dinner.

The guy usually called me once a week to bitch about some injustice at his job or some asshole who'd cut him off on the freeway. He had a temper, but who gave a damn?

He'd grown up in a working-class neighborhood with working-class parents. His dad was a plumber, and his mom was a postal worker. If he didn't have grit, the kids in his neighborhood would've beat the shit out of him.

"Your enemy's enemy is your friend," Rachel said to Eva. Eva glared at me.

"That doesn't make sense." Eva rolled her eyes.

"Trust me. He's on our side," Rachel said.

Rachel texted me earlier, told me she had a plan, and to meet them at the bar.

"You hate Joe, and you hate me," I said, hooking her hazel gaze with mine. "But I also hate Joe. Which means I'm your ally."

"What the hell are you talking about? Joe's your best friend," Eva said, but her voice stumbled over the last two words.

"You're not the only one Joe stabbed in the back," I said, my voice a low rumble.

"What the hell are you talking about?" Eva crossed her arms, but there was a touch of curiosity on her light features. "Is this a trap?

"No," I snapped. The emails I'd read between Jasmin and Joe skittered across my mind, and my mood turned black.

"Did he forget to call you on your birthday?" Eva mocked.

"He slept with Jasmin," I snarled, my fingers curling into a fist around my drink.

That shut her up. Eva didn't know much about my past relationships, but she knew about Jasmin.

"When?" Eva stuttered.

"A week after Jasmin broke up with me, his dick was inside her."

Eva flinched.

"Joe might still be fucking her if you hadn't come along."

Jasmin and I broke up right before Joe met Eva, although I didn't find out Joe slept with Jasmin until a month ago.

"You're lying." Eva was wide-eyed, clearly shocked by this news. "Joe would never do that to you."

Blood boiled under my skin, sweat prickling my lower back.

"It's true," Rachel said gently. "Ethan showed me the emails. That's why I knew we could trust him."

"Ethan's a tech genius. He could've faked those emails," Eva said, a tremble in her voice.

"I'm not lying," I fumed.

Her phone was on the bar, and I snatched it, clicking it on. I held it in front of her face, and when it unlocked, I opened her browser. I pulled up Joe's email server and logged in. Then I handed it to her.

"Is that Joe's email account?"

Eva frowned and scrolled through it.

"Yeah," she said warily.

"Search Jasmin's name."

She did, and the emails popped up. Her eyes scanned the emails, her hand covering her mouth as she read them.

"I may be a so-called tech genius," I said. "But I

can't magically put emails into someone's account, backdate them, and attach fake photos."

"Photos," she murmured, clicking on an attachment. She gasped and threw her phone at me like she'd been burned. I caught it and put it on the bar.

"That's why Ethan's here," Rachel said soothingly. "He's just as pissed as you are, but he hasn't said anything for your sake."

Eva's jaw hung down and she shook her head from side to side in disbelief.

"Fuck," she said, her eyes locking with mine. "It's one thing to betray me...but you? You're like Joe's brother."

"That's why I'm here." A fist of anger shoved into my throat, making my voice sound like it was scraping over gravel. "I want him to pay."

"What exactly do you think we're doing?" Eva challenged.

"Getting revenge on the bastard. That's why you're here, right? To make a plan and execute it." I smiled ruefully. "It's what you do best."

Eva's lips were drawn down, but the right side of her mouth twitched like she was holding back a smile.

I pulled a stool between the two women and sat.

"I bet you have an Excel file started already," I said.

A small smile unfurled on her face. "Maybe."

I knew it. The girl can't do anything without a spreadsheet.

I turned to the bartender and ordered shots. We took the three glasses of tequila and raised them.

"This goes no further than the three of us," I said, my heart thundering behind my ribs.

Eva clinked our shot glasses. There was a fire in her eyes, and it thrilled me. I'd never seen her this animated.

"To the revenge pact," Rachel said, and we threw back the shots.

Eva slammed her shot glass down so hard it shattered on the bar.

Yes, I definitely wanted to get to know this Eva much better.

# Chapter 6

## *Eva*

My vision board was gone. In its place was the revenge board.

I sat cross-legged on the California king bed Joe and I shared in our Washington Heights apartment. It was near the top of the island on 155th Street and Riverside Drive. If you leaned out the kitchen window, you could see a small sliver of the Hudson River.

It was a quiet, tree-lined street right next to a huge cemetery and mausoleum.

Maybe that was an omen of the death of our relationship.

We'd moved in a year ago, and most of Joe's boxes were still shoved together in a corner. I'd unpacked mine in the first week. I'd planned to surprise him and organize everything after the wedding craziness was done but screw him. He could unpack his own damn boxes.

Joe was upstate on a new job for the builder he worked for, making up for the time lost due to the wedding activities last month.

Typically, he took the hour-long train ride home each day, even if it was late. But there were issues at the new housing development, and he needed to be on-site from sunup to sundown, which in the summer meant most of the day.

Fine by me.

I'd been worried he was with Ashley, but she was at her Hamptons house share this week. Her Insta stories were filled with skimpy bikinis and boat rides and sunsets with cocktails.

A soft purring filled the room. Thor, our neighbor's fluffy white cat, was nestled on Joe's pillow next to me.

I snapped a picture of him and pressed print on my phone. The printer whirred to life and spit out a small photo of the cat. I cut it out, flipped it over, smeared glue on the back of the paper, and stuck it in the top right corner of the board.

There was a knock on the front door, and my nerves jumped under my skin. Thor mewed, then licked his paw and went back to sleep. I shoved the canvas under the bed and reminded myself there was nothing wrong with what I was doing. My new husband had been sticking his dick into another woman for months.

A little revenge was well-deserved.

I swung the heavy apartment door open, expecting my neighbor Lupe, but it was Ethan.

My smile dropped.

"What are you doing here?" I frowned.

The black running shorts and Dri-FIT top he wore hugged his body, and I tried not to be impressed by his well-defined muscles pushing through the tight fabric. His walnut-brown hair was disheveled, but despite the heat, he looked fresh and dry.

My hair was shoved into a messy bun, greasy and unkempt, and I wore an AC/DC T-shirt and boy-short underwear.

Ethan grinned, but there was tension at the corners of his mouth.

"I come bearing gifts." He lifted a small box in his hands. "I brought your favorite. Ladurée macarons."

I released the door, but Ethan stopped it with his designer tennis shoe and walked inside the small entryway.

It had been six days since I'd seen Ethan at the bar and he'd revealed Joe's second betrayal. After two years of animosity, it was unsettling having him in my apartment offering gifts.

"What do you want?" I crossed my arms, not taking the box of cookies.

He put it on the small table under the coat hooks.

"To plan the revenge stuff."

"I thought we'd just text our ideas. We don't need to meet IRL," I stated plainly, walking to the bedroom.

Ethan followed but stopped at the doorway, sweeping his gaze over the mess on the floor—scissors, glue sticks, scraps from the revenge article, photos of

Joe I'd taken and some of Ashley I'd printed from Insta, my laptop open with my revenge task list.

"Despite the pact, my trust in you is razor thin." I pulled my revenge board out from under the bed.

From the pile of photos, I picked up one of Ashley and placed it on the canvas, jabbing pushpins in her breasts and groin, securing it in place.

"Yikes." Ethan cringed.

"Shut up and start cutting." I handed him the magazine article. "We don't need to be chummy."

Ethan trimmed number eight from the article: "Have a Revenge Affair." He stared at it for a few beats and then slathered it with glue and stuck it on the board.

"Are you doing all of these?" he asked.

He continued to trim and paste, but his shoulders had tensed.

"Do you have a problem with some of them?" I asked, my skin prickling in defense. I didn't know if I'd ever trust him fully.

Ethan and Joe had been best friends since they were six. He'd practically lived at Joe's house because Ethan's parents sucked.

Joe's family was loud and rough around the edges but stable and loving. Their home had been Ethan's sanctuary from his dysfunctional parents. That's how Joe's parents had described it one night when we were all hanging out at their house.

"He's a liar." Ethan stood and crossed his arms over

his chest, staring down at me. "The bastard deserves all of this."

Yikes. It was during moments like this when he was all serious and unrelenting that I saw a glimpse of the man who ran a multimillion-dollar company.

Thor leaped off the bed, landing softly on his paws, and circled between Ethan's legs in a figure eight.

"You got a cat?" Ethan picked up the fluff ball and scratched him under his chin. Thor closed his eyes and leaned his face into Ethan's hand, luxuriating.

Some women might melt watching a handsome man cuddle a cat. Not me. It annoyed the crap out of me.

I gently pulled Thor from Ethan's arms, gave the cat a quick scratch on the head, and placed him back atop Joe's pillow. Thor circled twice, then settled back on his perch.

"Joe's allergic to cats," Ethan said, brushing the white fur from his charcoal top, the taut muscles in his forearms moving rhythmically.

"Precisely. It's the first item on my revenge list." I picked up my laptop and moused over to the Excel file, marking the task done. "I told my neighbor I was lonely without Joe here during the day and asked if Thor and I could keep each other company while she was at work. He wanders everywhere except the spare room, which is closed."

Ethan's dark brows pinched together. "Why not there?"

"So Joe will have a dander-free sanctuary away from me. He'll have to sleep on the futon bed in there to get any relief."

Ethan laughed. "Clever."

I shrugged.

"You don't hate Joe," I stated as I pasted a picture of rotting fish on the board. I hadn't figured out where I'd plant the frozen fish. I couldn't put it in his luggage. He'd know it was me. It had to be more subtle.

"Hate is too nice a word," Ethan grumbled.

"You might be mad at him, but you don't hate him."

Ethan sank to the floor and flipped through the stack of photos I'd printed: a broken heart, Viagra, Nair, burning clothes, spray paint cans.

"You're right," he said, his azure-hued eyes locking with mine. "I want Joe to realize he's turned into a selfish shit whose actions have consequences. Jasmin broke my heart, and Joe consoled me with six-packs and tickets to hockey games. I spent months wallowing in his apartment, all the while he was fucking her."

A shiver cascaded down my spine. "How serious was it?"

Sleeping with Jasmin a few times would be awful, but not as deceitful as an ongoing affair.

"He was with her for weeks."

The blood drained from my face.

Jasmin had wrecked Ethan when she dumped him. Joe said he turned from the nice guy he'd once been into the bitter man he'd become, but I never thought of

Ethan as bitter. Cautious, maybe, and a shithole to me, but not bitter.

"When did you find out about them?" I asked. "Hasn't it been like two years since you broke up?"

"A week before the wedding. I was looking up something for the best man speech on Joe's old email account. I still had access to it from when he'd been hacked and I needed to secure it for him."

Ethan was a whiz at IT, hence his award-winning app that made him a millionaire overnight when Yelp bought it.

"I stumbled on an email from Jasmin. It wasn't anything damning, but it was the familiarity and tone of the email that raised my suspicions. I was up all night debating if I could invade Joe's privacy, but there was something in my gut that knew. So I did a search, and hundreds of emails and chats appeared." Ethan's hands folded into fists, his features darkening. "They got together barely a week after the breakup. While I was punching the shit out of his sofa pillows and drinking my misery away, Joe was sneaking off and fucking her. And"—Ethan's voice rose—"I slept with Jasmin two more times after we split. *Fuck.*"

Ethan slammed his fists in his lap, a vein on his forehead pulsing under the skin.

"Oh God," I mumbled miserably. Had Joe been sleeping with other women the entire time we'd been together?

Ethan sensed this question—probably because my face had gone red hot with fury.

"He wasn't like that with you," Ethan said, his voice gentle. "He was devoted. He wouldn't even look at other women or comment on them after you two got together."

"You can't be sure," I snorted. "You had no idea he was sleeping with your ex right under your nose."

A thundercloud of emotion shadowed his face. "I'm sure of it because you guys didn't—"

Ethan cut himself off, his cheeks pink.

"What?" I asked.

"Shit."

"We didn't what?" I asked, biting into my bottom lip.

"You didn't have sex."

"We had sex!" I screeched, heat shooting up my neck. "We had a lot of sex."

At first.

And then school got busy and there was job hunting and graduation planning and then the move and the wedding. Sex had never been a priority in my life.

"Wouldn't that make him more likely to cheat?" I asked, not meeting Ethan's eyes, embarrassed to have to defend my sex life.

"Joe loves sex. It's all he talked about once he started having it," Ethan said. "If he stayed with you, despite the sex stuff, he obviously loved you."

"Until he didn't," I said, my voice faltering. Had it been that simple? Our sex life wasn't good enough for Joe, so he threw it all away?

"It's not your fault."

"I know that." I reared back, anger filling my voice.

"Forget I said anything," he grumbled.

He dropped to the rug and tugged the revenge board toward him.

I tugged it back.

"Why didn't you confront Joe?" I asked, standing up and putting distance between us, glad my sex life was no longer being discussed. "About Jasmin."

Ethan and I weren't friends. At best we were frenemies, and that was only because I'd had to tolerate him as Joe's best friend.

"You still don't trust me?" he asked.

"Nope." I crossed my arms. "You thought I was using Joe for a green card. You told him to dump me long before we were engaged."

Ethan shook his head, scowling. "Did you read all of Joe's private messages?"

I shrugged.

"Not on purpose. His laptop was always open and unlocked. I used it to turn in schoolwork sometimes, and it was kinda hard to ignore the messages when they were in the middle of the screen. Especially if I saw my name. I never snuck into his phone or anything. It was just there."

I sighed and reorganized the supplies in front of me.

"You wrote a lot of shitty things about me. You said I was cold and unfeeling, that I didn't love Joe, and that I was using him to stay in the country." I gathered and dumped the pens, tape, and tacks into my vintage Caboodle.

"You were wrong," I said, aggressively putting each item into a neat snack in its slot as I spoke.

"First. I had a student visa when I met Joe. I wasn't looking for a way to stay in America because I'd always planned to move back to Toronto after graduation. It wasn't until Joe and I discussed getting married that my plans shifted. Work was better for Joe in the States, and I'd fallen in love with Manhattan. It made sense to stay here.

"Second, I did love Joe—maybe I still do—but I'm an emotional cripple, okay? My father abandoned my mom and me for weeks. No text. No note. No goodbye. We'd wake up and he'd be gone. My mom would act like nothing was wrong while he was gone, and they never talked about it when he returned. It was a weird, robotic life. From the outside we looked normal, but inside it was a rotting mess."

I slammed the lid of the Caboodle shut.

"One ex called me a shell of a human," I snorted bitterly. "I may not have shown it in a way you approved, Ethan, but I adored Joe. He pushed me out of my comfort zone. I never went to parties or social events before him. He showed me New York City, and I fell in love with it."

Ethan sat quietly, his face unreadable as I word-vomited everything out. All the arguments that had been living in my head, keeping me up at night after I'd read those texts from Ethan.

"Joe's like a puppy." I smiled despite myself.

Ethan's mouth lifted into a small smile of agreement.

"He was always excited when he saw me. It was like I was the sun and he was the flower basking in my light. I felt loved. I'd never felt like that before."

My voice wobbled, and I swallowed over the lump in my throat, pushing the pain away.

"When he asked me to marry him, it meant I could have two things that I suddenly wanted desperately— to be loved by him and to live in New York where people know how to get stuff done."

When I finished, I fiddled with the pictures on the board, avoiding Ethan's eyes. I felt raw and vulnerable under his scrutiny.

"I didn't know all that," Ethan said, contrite.

"No, you didn't." I looked up. His brow was knitted in regret, but it disappeared and was replaced by something harsher.

"You never touched him." Ethan sighed. "He was eager for your attention, and you ignored him half the time. Joe wanted validation, something to show him you felt the same, but you were always buried in your phone organizing something, or going to a seminar, or planning your week. Do you ever live in the moment?"

"I'm living in the moment right now, unfortunately," I said, throwing my arms up. "Are you saying it's my fault he cheated?"

"No," Ethan said forcefully.

"Don't blame the victim," I scoffed, my muscles tightening.

"I'm not," Ethan barked.

We glared at each other, and the air between us crackled with tension, the only sound the rapid breathing through our noses.

"Show me the emails between Joe and Jasmin," I demanded. "Rehashing all this reminds me why I don't trust you."

Anger flashed behind Ethan's eyes.

"I already showed you," Ethan said.

"You showed me the time stamp. I want to see the words."

I lifted my eyebrows, waiting.

"Fine." He raised his phone, tapped on it, then turned it to me.

I read the email on the screen.

*Come to mine at 3. My roommate's at a study group all afternoon. I bought some edible massage oils ;) xoxo Jaz (delete this email)*

"He didn't delete it," I said lamely.

"He put them in a folder called Extra Credit. There were a lot of them. Click to the next one."

I read several more, and it became clear it was way worse than I imagined. This wasn't Joe screwing Ethan's ex once or twice. They'd had a full-fledged relationship. They even went on a weekend getaway together.

My hands were clammy, my skin hot. A shot of rage zipped through my veins, and I grabbed the revenge board and threw it across the room. It hit the wall, and the wood splintered with a satisfying *crack*. Thor hissed and ran out the door.

My chest tightened and I pressed my hand to it, trying to deepen my breaths.

"Was everything a lie?" The words tumbled out of my mouth in a panic. "Oh my God. I have to get tested! What if that slut gave me something?"

I opened the contacts on my phone, searching for my doctor, but my hands shook so bad I kept clicking the wrong name. Ethan pried the phone from my fingers and put his hand on my shoulder.

"Get the hell away from me," I roared and shoved him aside. My skin burned where he'd touched me.

"Breathe, Evelyn," Ethan said, keeping his distance, his hands up.

I sucked in a deep breath. Then another, the stars that obscured my vision clearing.

I sank to the bed, my head in my hands. I'd done a good job distracting myself with the revenge stuff, but the fact remained—I didn't know the man I married.

Ethan sat on the bed next to me, keeping a foot between us. He handed me the phone.

I tapped my nail on the screen, thinking.

"What is it?" he asked.

"I want to hurt him, Ethan. I want to hurt him as bad as he hurt both of us."

"I've got a few ideas." Ethan smiled wryly.

"I've got two ears and all night." I sat back and pulled the broken board toward me.

Ethan glanced at Thor, who slinked back into the room and lay across the pile of accouterment at our feet.

"We're gonna need to think a lot bigger than his cat allergies."

# Chapter 7

## *Eva*

Joe and I were tucked away in the corner of the W Hotel lounge on a white leather sofa. We couldn't afford it, but he'd ordered bottle service. The cheapest thing on the menu was Veuve, and it was over three hundred dollars.

Joe put his face in the crook of his elbow and sneezed several times. I shifted away. Sneeze droplets didn't mix with overpriced champagne.

"I've washed every damn sheet and towel." Joe snatched a napkin and sneezed into it. "What the hell?"

I sipped my champagne, avoiding his russet glare, the whites of his eyes pink from irritation.

The cat hair plan had worked perfectly, but even I was getting tired of Joe's wheezing and complaining. After this weekend, I was going to rent a carpet cleaner and deep clean all the rugs. Operation Cat was a success, but it needed to be over.

49

"Ugh." Joe dug his fingers into the top of his favorite trousers and tugged the waistband. They were cutting into his hips. "Keto starts tomorrow."

I smiled into my flute.

"It's not funny, Eva."

He unrolled the short sleeves of his white linen top, which cut into his biceps, and released a frustrated groan.

"Why is everything so tight?" he griped.

It was Ethan's idea to switch out Joe's favorite clothing items for the same exact ones but a size smaller. Joe had been a chubby kid and was obsessive about his workout regime and diet as an adult.

Earlier this week, Ethan inventoried Joe's clothes and brought a bag of new duplicate items over. I'd torn out the old tags with a seam ripper, sewed them into the smaller-sized items, and put them back in his drawers and closet.

It was a small victory when Joe pulled on his trousers tonight and his face collapsed.

"Fat and happy." I patted his flat stomach.

He shoved my hand off.

"I'm not fucking fat." He downed his drink and then poured another glass to the rim.

"Then happy." My smile was saccharine sweet, but he didn't notice the sarcasm.

"Sure, baby." He squeezed my hand dismissively.

If I hadn't discovered Joe's infidelity, would I have noticed his distance? Was Ethan right? Had I not been present in this relationship even when it was good?

I snuggled into Joe and looked up at him with a soft gaze, testing him. "It's not me, is it?"

He nuzzled his nose into my neck, kissing under my earlobe, and I leaned into his affection. The part of me that still loved Joe, that hadn't gotten the message that he was a cheating fuckhead, melted into the kiss. This was the part of me that wanted to forget what I knew, play pretend, and let everything go back to how it was.

Every day I woke up with my insides in knots, anxiety clawing at me, the panic reminders of my childhood. I used to lie in bed paralyzed, the stress of not knowing if my dad would return pressing against my chest until it felt like my ribs would break.

Mom and I would go about our day as if it were normal. Then he'd show up one day and they'd act like nothing happened. The one time I worked up the courage to ask them why Dad disappeared, they both looked at me, said nothing, then went back to eating as if I hadn't spoken.

Part of me wanted to hide from the truth of Joe's behavior like my mom had with my dad's, because I still cared about Joe.

Love wasn't a valve you could switch off when you wanted to, even if the person you gave your heart to destroyed it.

Then there was the part of me that burned with an inferno of hate and wanted to tear his dick off.

Joe's phone buzzed, and I mentally shook the ick from my head.

He glanced at the screen and I studied his scalp. I'd decided not to use Nair in Joe's shampoo since his head was still shaved but little sprouts of hair had filled in everywhere.

"Are you letting your hair grow out?" I asked.

"Uh, yeah," he said, distracted by his phone.

I made a note that if he didn't shave it again, I'd use Nair.

He scowled as he read his screen.

"What is it?" I asked.

"A Google notification."

"About what?" I leaned over. Joe darkened his screen, but not before I saw the headline. It was something about Ethan and his foundation.

I rolled my eyes. Of course, Joe would have a Google alert set up about Ethan. He'd been so weird about Ethan ever since he sold his app.

Despite my disdain for Ethan, I respected his career and everything he'd done with his success.

When I met him, he'd just launched the app, Potty Please. It surprised everyone, including Ethan, when the app quickly became number one.

The app was a crowd-sourcing program that started out as a parents' helper to locate bathrooms, changing stations, and places to nurse in any city around the world.

The idea had stemmed from Ethan's sister, Savi, who had just had a baby girl and was pissed at the lack of places to change and nurse her in Manhattan. Especially in the middle of winter when Savi couldn't sit down on a park bench and do all the things without freezing the baby's bits off.

After the launch, the app expanded to include the locations of all types of public bathrooms, not just for parents. Each one was rated by location, cleanliness, and convenience and had pictures and written reviews.

A year after it launched, Yelp swooped in, bought the app, and integrated it into their system.

It made Ethan a shit ton of money, but he used most of it to open his foundation.

I'd been impressed and annoyed when I found out about the foundation. It was exactly the type of company I wanted to run one day. It provided resources and programs for children, teens, and young adults that were troubled or needed a leg up.

The foundation, Coding for Change, focused on teaching coding at after-school and big brother/sister-type programs. The foundation also teamed up with tech companies, which gave the teens and adults internships and jobs once they completed the coding courses.

I'd done a deep dive into the company after Ethan opened it. If he hadn't hated me, I would've applied for a job there.

Joe grumbled anytime someone brought up Ethan's accomplishments. I'd always made excuses for Joe's bitterness toward Ethan's success, but now I saw it for what it was.

Jealousy. Pure and simple.

Joe's phone beeped. He read the text, then turned toward the entrance and waved.

Walking toward us was Ethan, frowning. The scowl on his face deepened when his gaze landed on me, cozy against Joe's side.

My belly twisted nervously as if I were doing something wrong, but I had to keep up the pretense of a happy relationship for this to work.

Joe handed Ethan one of the champagne flutes, and Ethan sat down on the arm of the white sofa next to me, drinking the contents of his champagne flute, never taking his eyes off mine.

I gulped water, my heart pounding.

It was the first time the three of us were together since Ethan and I were in cahoots. It was weird.

I shifted, confused by the bubbling heat that swirled around my chest when he looked at me that intensely. I felt close to him in a way that was soothing and unbearable all at once.

I guess holding a secret between two people did that.

# Chapter 8

## *Ethan*

When Joe texted and told me to meet him out for a drink, I didn't know he meant with Eva. My skin felt tight and itchy with her so close after spending the past week planning and plotting together.

In the middle of her sewing the tags into the smaller clothing I'd bought, I caught myself staring at her, replaying everything she'd told me about her parents and her view of her relationship with Joe.

Joe slid his hand over Eva's thigh and massaged it. Her hand clasped his, and she brought it to her lips, kissing his fingers lightly.

"I didn't know you were meeting us out tonight." Eva raised her gaze to me casually.

"Joe invited me," I said, the low bass of the moody soul music vibrating the soles of my shoes.

Joe slapped me on the back and said, "I can't let my man hide away in his palace getting blue balls forever."

I coughed out a shocked laugh. "What the hell, man?"

"What?" Joe raised his hands in the air, all innocence. "You haven't banged a girl in like a year."

"Nice, Joe." Eva rolled her eyes.

"I'm getting a drink." I glanced at the champagne bottle and threw in the next bit to annoy Joe. "A real drink."

Joe's shoulders tensed, but his voice was light when he said, "When you exude masculinity like me, it doesn't matter what you drink." Then a beat. "Grab us some shots. The good stuff."

I walked away but heard Joe bang his flute on the table and scoff, "He can afford it."

My jaw tightened. When Joe felt threatened, he lashed out. I knew this about him, but no one was without their faults. Joe had an inferiority complex because he'd grown up with working-class parents and went to a trade school instead of college.

But the man had drive. I'm sure that's what first drew Eva to him. She met him right after he'd attended some Tony Robbins knockoff seminar and he was all fired up.

Joe had his goals written down and labeled and a spreadsheet with all the steps necessary to achieve each one. The morning after I met Eva, she was hovering over Joe's shoulder, looking at his mapped-out life.

Joe's goal had been to get a job on a construction crew for an established builder, work his way up to site manager, and one day run his own construction company.

But something had shifted in Joe a year ago after the Yelp deal. I lost friends and gained wannabes once that money hit my bank account, and Joe became guarded and defensive whenever the mention of money came up.

Now, as I approached the seating area with the shots, I heard Joe say, "Where's the waitress? I want to order some Macallan."

Eva grabbed Joe's wrist and hissed, "We're not spending hundreds of dollars just to prove a point."

He shook her off. "It's my money. I can do what I want."

This was Joe at his worst. Self-loathing and odious.

I rounded the leather sofa and slid the tray of shots on the table, glass clinking. I grunted cheers and raised the shot but stopped halfway to my mouth.

Ashley sashayed toward our group dressed in a tight dress that looked like it was made of red rubber bands sewn together.

"Ashley," Eva said with a forced smile. "What a surprise."

"Really?" Ashley giggled, but there was something devious in the lilt of her voice. "Joe asked me to come."

Joe's eyebrows shot up, and his gaze bounced between the four of us.

"For Ethan," he blurted, recovering, and I shot a dark look at Joe. What the hell was he talking about?

Ashley balked, her mouth pulling into a pout.

I exchanged a glance with Eva, a thought rocketing between us. *Was she here to blow everything up like she'd tried to do at the wedding?*

Eva shook her head back and forth subtly, the message clear. *We have to stop her.*

"Ashley doesn't look like she needs any help from us when it comes to men," I purred, handing her my shot, hoping to diffuse the situation. "You're gorgeous as always."

Ashley sidled next to me, dipping her tongue into the drink, and wet her lips with the liquid. "A man with good taste."

I winked, and we threw the shots back. A drop of liquid slid down Ashley's chin, and I wiped it away with my thumb. She caught my palm and stuck the tip of my thumb in her mouth, slowly sucking on it.

Joe snatched the final shot and drank it, glowering.

"I'll get another round," I said.

"I'll come with you." Ashley hooked her arm in the crook of my elbow.

My goal was to distract her from Joe and whatever fire they were playing with.

Ashley leaned over the bar, the bottom of her butt cheeks poking out of her dress. Two perfectly round globes, but I had no interest in her. Ashley only ever thought of herself.

Back at the table, Eva picked up one of the cloudy shots we'd brought over and swirled it around.

"What is it?" she asked.

"A lemon drop."

We all clinked glasses and drank another round, my head spinning. They were sweet, but there was a bitter aftertaste that clung to the tongue.

Ashley plonked next to me and put her hand on my thigh. "I bet it gets lonely in that big loft of yours. Are you like Hugh Grant in that *About a Boy* movie? A man alone all day on his island of one?"

I laughed, pretending the comment wasn't offensive. My life wasn't a waste. I paid my luck forward every day at the foundation.

"Something like that."

"I'd be happy to pack my bathing suit and join you anytime you get bored."

Damn. This woman was not subtle.

Joe coughed beside me.

"Er..." I squirmed, uncomfortable with how close Ashley's hand was to my crotch. "I'm busy with my nonprofit most days."

Ashley scooted closer, her thigh pressing against my leg. "You smell nice. What is that?" she cooed.

"Soap."

Eva covered a laugh, and Ashley shot her a look of annoyance.

"How's the foundation?" Eva asked, leaning forward.

"We've expanded the training beyond coding and now include classes on basic business skills and marketing. I'm teaming with tech companies to come in and mentor the kids."

"That's awesome." She gaped and looked flustered.

"Eva's starstruck because that's what she wants to do." Joe laughed as if it were a joke. "Manage a do-gooder foundation. But you don't really do anything. You have a whole staff of people at the foundation that actually run it."

Joe liked to think I spent my days aimlessly spending my money on expensive hobbies like kite surfing and mountain biking and adventure retreats. I did those things sometimes, but most days I worked with my team at the company.

"Those are some lucky kids," Ashley said, her voice husky.

Joe sneezed several times, hacking into a cocktail napkin.

"Is it warm in here?" He rubbed his neck, his breathing labored and wheezy.

"Joe," Eva said, grabbing his shoulders. His eyelids lolled, his eyes rolling back.

"Ethan!" She swung her alarmed gaze to me, and I was by her side in a heartbeat. "Something's wrong."

Before I could inspect him, Ashley shoved me aside.

"Hold the light up," she directed.

Eva raised the flashlight on her phone, illuminating his face and neck.

Ashley pressed her fingers to his pulse and listened to his breathing. Ashley was a veterinarian, specializing in large animals. She wasn't a human doctor, but her command of the situation made me sit back and let her lead.

"Ethan, find security. Tell them we need help," Ashley directed over her shoulder, sitting Joe up.

"I'm fine." Joe batted her off weakly.

"Are you allergic to anything?" she asked.

"Cats," Joe said.

"No. Like food," she clarified.

"Eggs," Eva said, her voice thick with fear. "It's not deadly, but...this is worse than I've ever seen it."

Two large men in security uniforms barreled over to our small group. Ashley instructed them to help her walk Joe outside and directed me to hail a taxi. Eva trailed after. Joe could walk, which was a good sign, but he was shaky.

At the curb, I held the door of a yellow cab open, and Ashley slid in next to Joe. Eva tried to go in with them, but Ashley slammed the door.

"You two get the next one. Meet us at Mount Sinai."

The cab flew forward, and Eva jumped back, slamming into my chest.

One of the security guys hailed another cab, and I pulled Eva in. We zipped across Broadway in silence, processing what had just occurred.

We pulled up outside the hospital and raced into the emergency room, whipping our heads around and searching for Ashley and Joe.

"Can I help you?" an older woman asked, adjusting her bright teal glasses.

"Yes," Eva said. "A woman with black hair just came in with a man who was having an allergic reaction."

The receptionist cocked her scarf-covered head. "What's his name?"

"Joseph Patell. They would've come in five minutes before us. Just now."

The receptionist raised her gaze over her computer screen. "No one's come through these doors in the last half hour."

Eva and I exchanged a look. "Is there another entrance? Somewhere else they would've come in?"

The nurse told us to hold on. Eva paced in front of the desk.

"Did they get into an accident on their way here? Did he asphyxiate in the cab and they had to pull over to help him?" Eva spoke to herself, the words tumbling out.

"I'm sorry, but we have no patients by that name. Perhaps they went to another hospital?"

Eva's mouth opened and closed like a fish out of water. I steered her toward a hard, plastic chair.

"Do you have Ashley's number?" I asked.

Eva nodded.

"Call her. I've already sent a text and called Joe in the cab. No answer."

Eva tried Ashley, but it went straight to voice mail.

Then she texted her. And called her again. Then I tried Joe. It rang and rang.

Eva gripped her hands to her chest, her breathing short and fast.

"What if he's on the side of the road dying?" Eva said, clawing my shirt. "What if that bitch is there instead of me?"

She turned an accusing glare at me. "Did you do this?"

I rocked backward as if she'd hit me in the chest with her accusation. "No way."

"I wanted him to pay, but I didn't want to hurt him. Not like this." Her voice rose, squeaking on the last word.

"Is everything all right?" the receptionist asked, her eyebrow cocked wearily.

I guided Eva out to West Fifty-Ninth Street and down the block to a quieter street.

"Are you lying to me?" she asked through gritted teeth.

"I didn't do this." My fingers dug into her shoulders, frustrated that she'd accuse me. "Take a breath. Ashley probably told us the wrong hospital. Or we misunderstood. There are several Mount Sinai locations." I raised my phone. "I'll start with the first one, you take the second. We'll go down the list until we find them."

She seemed to like this. It was a task, something to do.

We went through the list one by one. When we got

to the last one, we still hadn't found Joe, but her breathing had steadied.

We sat on the stoop of a brownstone, and my mind whirled around the possibilities. My hand hurt from gripping the phone.

"I didn't do this," I said again, my gaze on the ground. "And you didn't do this."

"No," she confirmed. "Maybe it was something in the shots."

"Egg in shots?" I raised an eyebrow.

"Probably not," she said.

I grabbed the stone siding of the stoop and bent forward, my head between my biceps as realization dawned on me.

"Fuck!" I pushed off.

"What?" Eva flinched at my outburst.

"Something's not right," I said "I think this was deliberate."

"I didn't do it!" she yelled. A woman walking her dog stepped off the curb to avoid us.

"I know that!" I yelled back. Why was she always so damn combative?

We glared at each other.

"Then who?" she huffed. "Ashley?"

She said it as a joke, but my eyes widened.

"Would she be that crazy?" I asked.

"It doesn't make sense."

"Except here we are. Without them," I said. "And they're God knows where. Alone."

"But he's sick."

"Is he?" I asked.

Eva gasped.

It was insane, but if I hadn't done this to Joe, and Eva hadn't done this to him, maybe no one had.

Maybe he was faking it.

# Chapter 9

## *Eva*

"Do you really believe Joe would fake an allergy attack just to be with Ashley?" I asked, wrapping my head around Ethan's accusation.

We were in an Uber flying down the Bowery on our way to Ashley's apartment. When we couldn't locate Joe in any hospitals, we debated where they would've gone. They were too broke to go to a hotel, and it would be stupid for them to go to Joe's and my place. Ashley's was the logical choice.

I'd texted Rachel, and she'd sent me the address. It was on the south side of the Manhattan Bridge on the Lower East Side.

I held my stomach, sick at the thought that Joe would go to this length to trick me so he could be with her.

Tears blurred my vision, and I turned fully to my window, not wanting Ethan to see. He'd only use it against me later. Yeah, he was fully on my side when it came to getting back at Joe, but Ethan could barely stand to be near me before we came up with this pact.

Ethan was squeezed as far on the other side of the car as he could get, as if being in a closed space with me was unbearable.

Fine by me. I didn't want his cooties either.

"We'll find out soon enough," Ethan said, answering my question.

I felt his gaze on the back of my head, but I didn't turn around. The squat buildings rushed by as my fingers gripped the door handle. When we almost hit the river, the driver stopped, and we got out and followed my GPS until we stood in front of a five-story, red-brick, pre-war apartment complex. Outside the front entrance was a young woman with a braided pink fauxhawk, biker shorts, knee pads, and roller skates.

Rachel.

"I told you not to come," I said.

"Are you kidding me?" She circled Ethan and me on the narrow sidewalk. "I don't want to hear the watered-down story afterward. Besides, my game doesn't start for another hour, and this will pump me up."

Rachel was on the Brooklyn roller derby team. Her alter ego name on the team was Rebel Ray. Typically I'd be in the front row cheering her on, but my life had been so topsy-turvy I hadn't been to a game in weeks.

"So what are you going to do?" Rachel dug into the

sidewalk with the toe stop of her skate, halting by the door.

"Where's her apartment located?" Ethan glanced up at the building.

Rachel skated to the side next to a narrow pathway and pointed upward. "Fourth floor. Those are her windows overlooking the fire escape."

The light was off inside, and I didn't know if I was relieved or disappointed. Part of me wanted an answer to explain their disappearance, because no matter what they told me later, I wasn't going to believe their story.

"We can't knock on the door and catch them together because they can't know I know." I looked at the other buildings around us and the cars that lined the quiet block.

"You could hide and wait for them to exit," Rachel suggested, winding between Ethan and me.

"I want evidence," I said, heat creeping up my back. "Joe will deny it when I finally confront him, and I want to watch his face drop when I show it to him."

"Damn, girl." Rachel skidded sideways, stopping. "You sure you can handle seeing them without killing 'em?"

"Will you help me bury the bodies if I do?"

"Yep," Rachel said without hesitation.

I walked to the fire escape, but Ethan grabbed my arm before I could snatch the ladder.

"Are you sure you want to see them together? Those images will be burned in your brain," he said, and his tone suggested he knew this from experience.

I shoved my arm upwards and grabbed the rung, Ethan's hand falling away. "Everything already burns."

I pulled but the ladder didn't budge. I tried again, my muscles groaning at the effort.

"May I?" Ethan raised his arms, and with one yank it rolled down easily. Rachel and I exchanged a look, impressed by his Herculean strength.

Rachel skated to the corner of the building. "I'll keep a look out and text if there's any trouble or if I see them."

"I'll go first," I said.

Before Ethan could argue, I lifted my heeled foot onto the first rung and began the climb.

"Dammit, Evelyn. Really?"

I glanced down. Ethan's head was ducked, and he shook it in exasperation. It took me a moment, and then I knew what had caused this reaction. I wore a wrap dress, my lace underwear barely covering my butt cheeks.

"You've seen my ass before," I said, hoisting myself up to the second floor. "On my wedding day."

He cleared his throat. "This angle is a little different."

I smiled to myself, enjoying his discomfort, and clambered onto the platform. The windows were dark and the curtains were drawn, and I motioned for Ethan to climb up. Two more floors to go. Luckily, there were narrow steps instead of a ladder between the other floors.

I climbed a few steps, and a little white dog came

bounding down. It yapped, and I quickly picked it up and petted its puff of hair, trying to keep it quiet. It wiggled from my hands, scurried down the metal steps, and jumped around Ethan's legs. Its little body wrapped around his ankle, and the dog's hips ground into Ethan.

"Ugh. He's humping me." Ethan picked the little guy up, the small dog fitting easily in his palm. "Oh God!"

Ethan nearly dropped the dog but saved him at the last moment.

"What?" I asked, stepping back to the second-floor platform.

"What's that?" Ethan's face was screwed up in disgust.

My hands clamped over my mouth, covering my laugh. "A puppy penis."

"I know that," Ethan snapped, holding the fur ball away from his body. "But why is it all smooth and pink? I thought they were short and furry."

I bit my lips until I could answer without laughter. "It's called a lipstick."

"A what?!" Ethan cried, his eyes bulging.

"Shh," I said, gently taking the dog from Ethan and carrying it up to the third floor where it came from. The apartment on this level was also dark, but the window was cracked six inches, with just enough space for the doggie to get in and out.

I glanced down the steps where Ethan stared at his pant leg. "There's a wet spot. Do you think he—"

"Come on. We'll talk about the anatomy of dogs and semen later."

Ethan made a fake vomit noise. He seized my shoulders when he arrived, using me as a shield between him and the dog, which bounced around us on its paws before resting on a folded blanket.

"Ashley's floor is next," I said, the humor of the past few minutes rushing away.

Ethan stayed behind me, his hands on my shoulders, and we went up together. My head poked through the opening to the platform. There were two tall windows with no blinds or curtains that looked into a small bedroom, the double bed shoved against the wall under the windows.

I released my breath. The bed was empty. The room was dark, but the bedroom door was open, a light shining in from the hallway.

"They're not here," I said. Ethan scooted and sat next to me. "At least not in this room."

It was definitely Ashley's apartment. Her knockoff Louis Vuitton clutch was on the tall dresser—the L's too small, the V's too big—next to a pile of knotted headbands she loved to wear.

I glanced down at Rachel and I gave a thumbs-down, indicating they weren't here. A text buzzed on my phone.

*See anything?*

*Bedroom empty. Maybe they're in the living room or not here?* I texted Rachel back.

Light suddenly flooded onto the fire escape. Two

people stumbled into the room, laughing and kissing. The woman's shirt was off, and the man was undoing his pants.

I gasped, and Ethan clamped his palm over my mouth. With his other hand against my chest, he shoved me flat on my back, the length of his body spread on top of mine. There was a foot of wall below the windows hiding us.

Above our heads, the window slid open, and I heard Ashley's giggling voice through the crack. "The landlord always keeps it too hot in here, and we're about to steam it up."

Then she squealed and the bed springs creaked, her laughter drifting out the window.

"Damn. Your breasts are gorgeous," Joe said.

I froze, my heart leaping so hard I thought it might fly out of my chest. Ethan was flush against my front, the metal grate digging into my back, but I didn't care. Every nerve was on high alert as I listened to the sounds that came from above us.

"Better than her baby tits," Ashley said, and they both laughed.

My blood pumped like a rocket engine, the daggers of my humiliation striking me all over my body. I thrashed under Ethan. I had to get out of there. I couldn't listen to this. I'd die if I had to hear them make love.

"Let go," I hissed at Ethan because he wouldn't let me up.

"They'll see you," Ethan whispered roughly in my ear.

My head rocked back and forth as I tried to shut out the moans that pierced my ears, but I could hear every little sound of pleasure.

Tears poured out of my eyes.

"I can't take it," I whimpered, helpless.

"Tell me how bad you want this pussy," Ashley said roughly.

Ethan's palms clamped over my ears, and all sound disappeared. He squeezed my skull, and I shut my eyes, trying to disappear. His forehead was against mine, his breath moist against my creek.

With my ears covered, the sound of my blood pumping in my head lulled me into a calmer place. I felt like I was floating. My senses were skewed, and I had no idea what to feel or what was real in this blackness.

And then the truth slapped me: *a foot away, my shitty husband had his dick in another woman.*

More tears leaked out. Ethan's weight was an anchor, his hands a shield, his presence a comfort during one of the worst moments of my life.

I don't know how much time had passed when Ethan slid off me and released my ears. My body was covered in sweat and grit. My satin dress clung to me, and I stared at the grate above, my adrenaline seeping from my body. I shivered despite the warm night.

"Are you okay?" Ethan whispered.

I cut my gaze at him, the message clear. *Of course, I'm not fucking okay.*

Ethan shut his eyes in a long blink and nodded in understanding.

"They left the room for a snack," he said, crawling to the steps. I followed behind him in a crouch, my legs wobbly. I barely made it down the ladder, and on the last rung, I slipped, landing awkwardly on my right foot.

"Ah!" I cried out, pain shooting into my toes.

Rachel glided to me in a flash.

"Eva!" Rachel dropped to her padded knees and helped me sit up. "You look like you've been to war and back."

"She has," Ethan growled.

"They were having sex," I said, my voice cracking on the last word.

"Oh shit." Rachel gathered me in a tight hug.

"I'm okay," I said. It was a lie. We all knew it.

Ethan helped me stand, but I pushed him away. My trust in all humanity was shattered.

"I hate everyone," I said, hobbling on my injured foot. Rachel put a hand on my elbow, gliding next to me. I smiled weakly at her. "Except you."

I swung my gaze at Ethan. "I want the truth from you. Right now."

He eyed me wearily. "What truth?"

"Did you know about Joe and Ashley?"

"No."

"But you suspected."

"Yes," Ethan admitted. "I didn't know what exactly was going on, but Joe started talking about Ashley and reminiscing about when they'd been together. I got suspicious."

"You must have been relieved."

Ethan slid his gaze away. "I wasn't. I—"

"Bullshit," I ground out, and Ethan whipped his head back to me. He looked like he wanted to murder someone.

Ah...there was the Ethan I knew. The man who always had a chip on his shoulder when I was around. Who grumbled and spoke one-word answers.

"You said I wasn't good enough for him. You wanted him to dump me." I shot my first arrow.

Ethan's mouth gaped, and I could see the wheels in his head turning, remembering that I'd read the texts. "You're misremembering."

"Rachel." I raised my brow at her, and she lifted her phone, pulling up the screenshots of the texts I'd sent her when I'd first read them.

"*Dude, don't be a fool,*" Rachel read. "*The bimbo is using you.*"

Ethan leaped forward, reaching out to snatch the phone.

"No," he said, panicked, but Rachel dipped from his outstretched hand and glided away, too fast on her skates for him to catch her.

"*I saw a creepy poster in her bag. It was covered in pictures of the U.S. and you and a wedding dress. She's nuts.*"

Ethan glared at me. "You shouldn't have read those."

"Well, I did."

"All that stuff...it wasn't about you," Ethan said, his teeth grinding.

"What was it about?" I asked, heat shooting into my words, angry for so many reasons.

"It was about me, okay?" Ethan shoved his hands in his hair, tugging at the roots. "I was still hurting from my breakup with Jasmin."

I barked out a humorless laugh. "Were you hurting when you told Joe that marrying me would be the stupidest thing he'd ever done?"

"Fuck." He slammed his fists into the side of the building.

"And then you laughed. Both of you!" I shouted, and Rachel spun in front of me, trying to hush me. "It was the most humiliating moment of my life. Until now."

"I'm so sorry, Evelyn." His face contorted, anger and regret swirling through his features. "Please. It wasn't about you."

"So you said." I flung my hands out, shoving him—and Joe and all the lies and deceptions—away from me. I knew I was being harsh to Ethan, heaping him in with Joe's sins, but hearing those texts again was the reminder I needed.

Ethan had been my false savior these past weeks—from my wedding day up until he covered my ears under those windows—but Ethan wasn't here to help me.

Sure, he was working with me to hurt Joe, but I didn't want revenge anymore.

I wanted war.

# Chapter 10

## *Eva*

I sat across from Joe at our beat-up kitchen table, stabbing my steak with my fork. Nothing about this meal was appetizing, but on Sunday nights we had a standing dinner date at home.

I'd hoped our weekly dinner would conveniently slip Joe's mind since he was preoccupied with other things these days—namely, Ashley's vagina—but he'd bought the meal and cooked it as always.

A burning lump pressed in my throat, and I swallowed a large gulp of red wine over it. A raging inferno had been swirling in my veins since Friday after I'd been flat out on that fire escape listening to my husband screwing his mistress.

My knife sliced through the meat, scraping the plate.

"Damn, Eva. What did that piece of meat ever do to you?" Joe chortled at his joke.

"More than you know," I mumbled, shoveling a

large piece dripping with red juice into my mouth. It was tasteless.

"Hey, is this about Friday? I told you. By the time we got to the hospital, I was fine. False alarm. I made sure Ashley got home safely and then I came back here." Joe wiped his mouth with a cloth napkin which was part of a set someone had bought us for our wedding. They were off-white and already ruined from the red wine and A-1 sauce.

I gripped my wineglass in both hands and sat back, pushing my hardly touched plate aside.

"Not hungry?" Joe asked, sliding his fork through the sauce and scooping up a bite of potatoes au gratin... his favorite. This entire meal was his favorite.

He chose the meals on Sundays. I'd never minded because it was one less decision I had to make after a week of decision overload at work and home.

Now I saw it for the selfish thing it was—Joe only considering his own desires.

"I had a late lunch at DIG after I left Housing Works this afternoon." I paused. "With Carlos Rioja. Remember him?"

I sipped my wine and smiled blandly like I hadn't just dropped a bomb.

Carlos Rioja had been a classmate at Syracuse University and taught Argentine tango on the side. Me and half the student body—male and female—took his classes. He was new to the States, and I invited him out to drinks with friends one night after a lesson.

When Joe showed up and saw me with Carlos, he

was irate. It was the first time Joe had been possessive. He'd made it clear he didn't want me to take the classes anymore, but I told Joe to drop the machismo and continued.

Two weeks later, Joe signed us up for weekly kayaking adventures. And guess when the outings were? Yup. At the same time as the tango lessons.

Nothing got under Joe's skin more than his manhood being threatened. And I had a feeling if Joe caught me with someone the way I'd caught him with Ashley, he would go insane.

But I needed to test my theory. I wasn't a hundred percent confident that he'd still get jealous over me.

I zeroed in on Joe's reaction at my mention of Carlos. His fork had stilled halfway to his mouth, sauce dripping down the silverware and splattering on the plate.

"You had a lunch date with Carlos?" Joe snarled, his eyes narrowing. Inside, I sighed with relief. Joe was still threatened at the thought of another man wanting me.

"It wasn't a date." I giggled as if it was the silliest thing I'd heard. "I ran into him and we were both hungry, so we had something to eat. It was great to catch up. He's been teaching classes at a studio off Lafayette in SoHo."

"And..." Joe ground out through his teeth.

"He looked ah-mazing. He's still got that sexy Latino thing going for him. I bet every one of his students has a crush on him."

Joe slammed his palms on the table, the dishes clattering and the wine sloshing in the glasses. "I don't want you to see him again."

My heart ticked up a beat. I expected Joe to be irritated but not aggressive. Keeping a neutral expression, I lifted my phone and pretended to scroll through it.

"What are you looking at? Did you hear me?"

I lifted my gaze to his. "I was just checking we hadn't traveled back in time to the fifties when being a misogynistic ape was all the rage."

Joe sucked his lower lip into his mouth and bit down on it, thinking. He did this when he was recalibrating his strategy if his approach to a situation wasn't working to his advantage.

"I don't trust him." Joe lifted a shoulder in a half-shrug, downplaying his outburst, but a vein pulsed in his neck, and I knew he was pissed.

"Oh, Joe," I purred. "Don't be so juvenile. Do you really think someone could pull me away from you so easily? You act like you're inadequate."

I dropped my smile and doubt skittered across his face.

"I'm not fucking inadequate. I'm—"

"I think you were onto something Friday night," I cut him off, maneuvering the conversation in a new direction while his hackles were up. "We should set Ethan and Ashley up. In fact, we have that coupon for the spa weekend in the Catskills that you can't go to because of work. You know, the trip my mother gave us as a wedding present. We should give it to them."

Joe blinked rapidly, trying to catch up after my quick subject change. "Hell no, I don't want him near her—wait, I'm not done talking about Carlos. I—"

I batted my hand in front of me like I was batting away his worry. "Relax. Carlos is leaving the country next week for the fall. Forget I mentioned it. I didn't realize it was such a sensitive topic." Joe fumed across the table, and I barreled on. "Tell me why you don't want Ethan and Ashley to go out. I thought you were trying to set them up. I saw the way they were flirting. If your allergic reaction hadn't interrupted them, they may have sealed the deal that night."

Joe shook his head like there were too many thoughts crowding his mind. I was purposely throwing things at him rapidly to try and get honest reactions out of him.

A good general always does her due diligence before she goes into battle. And right now, I was behind enemy lines mining Joe for his greatest weakness.

"Ashley isn't into Ethan. She told me on Friday." Joe sat back, relaxing for a moment, no doubt feeling as if he was finally gaining some control back.

"Really? Huh." I pretended to consider this. "Wait. I know! Ethan and I should go away that weekend, then." I smiled brightly like this wasn't a ludicrous idea.

"You can't go with Ethan!" Joe roared, his neck muscles bulging, floundering again.

"Why not? I'd hate to see it go to waste, and you're

82

always busy and he's so generous." I gave Joe my best wide-eyed Bambi look.

"Because he's my best friend. And we're married! You can never fucking be with him. Why would you even say that? You can't—"

I broke into a smile, and Joe stopped midrant.

"You're joking," he said, his shoulders dropping. His wineglass was three-fourths full, but he finished it in two gulps. "You're in a funny mood tonight."

I cleared the plates, poured Joe another glass, and then snuggled into his lap, satisfied that I'd confirmed the best track for my ultimate revenge.

"It's been a while since we fucked," I whispered into his ear, nibbling the lobe. "Our little argument has me all riled up."

Joe usually initiated sex, but I needed to soothe his ego after what I'd just put him through, so I let him think I was hot for him and that this was all some kinky sex game I was playing.

"Who are you and what have you done with my wife?" Joe snatched me up and carried me to our bed. He kissed me and I held my breath, trying not to cringe.

I pressed my palm to his chest and pulled back.

"What's wrong?" He kissed my collarbone.

"It's the onions." I slid to the edge of the bed. "Let's brush our teeth and then continue."

Joe frowned, but he was extra sensitive when it came to hygiene. "Okay."

In the bathroom, I brushed my teeth quickly, then

leaned my shoulder against the doorjamb and said to Joe in a sultry voice, "Give me a few minutes. I'm gonna put on one of those barely there nighties I got at my bachelorette party."

I locked the door of the bedroom while Joe remained in the bathroom and put on the least sexy piece of lingerie I'd received. From under the bed, I pulled out a small container with tiny holes poked in the top. I popped the lid off and shook it upside down over Joe's pillow until several small spiders tumbled out. Then I slid the container back under the bed.

There was no way in hell I was sleeping with Joe. I'd picked up the container from the pet store earlier that day in anticipation of this moment.

Spiders didn't bother me, but Joe hated them. These were harmless and barely the size of a dime, but he wouldn't be able to relax thinking of them crawling around the room once he saw them.

Tonight had been carefully planned. Get inside Joe's head. Confirm his weakness. Then retreat.

I'd been in a tailspin ever since the fire escape. I couldn't get the sounds of him with Ashley out of my head. Before Ethan had saved me and blocked out the noises, I'd heard their moans, heard Ashley tell Joe to fuck her, heard them talk about my baby boobs.

When Joe came home and lied to my face an hour later, something broke in me, and over the past two days, I'd been on a mission to figure out what would destroy Joe to his core.

I hadn't spoken to Ethan since I'd lashed out at

him, but despite everything, I needed him on my side. I was gonna have to apologize, but one step at a time.

Switching out Joe's clothing tags and triggering his cat allergies was child's play. Joe was fucking with my entire life, jeopardizing my career, turning my existence into a joke.

Not to mention breaking my heart.

I swiped at a tear that ran unbidden down my cheek.

I didn't lie about running into Carlos, but we never had lunch. We'd said hi in passing and then went our separate ways. But seeing him today reminded me of Joe's jealousy and an idea hatched.

Joe was never gonna stop being a selfish prick. Ethan and I weren't going to be the last people he callously deceived, and before he could ruin anyone else, he deserved a taste of his own medicine.

A giant helping of it.

It was time to put on my big-girl revenge panties, and nothing would drive Joe more insane than catching me in bed with the one person he would never suspect of betraying him...

His childhood best friend.

The only hitch—I had to convince Ethan.

# Chapter 11

## *Eva*

My hand hovered over the buzzer of Ethan's apartment. It was a five-story, pre-war building in Nolita. Originally it had been a carriage house and later became a candle factory before developers got their hands on it and converted it into luxury, loft-style apartments. Ethan lived on the top floor.

I read up on the history when I googled the address, readying for this phase of the revenge games. I mapped out my strategy, timed my arrival for when Ethan would most likely be home, put on a subtly sexy sundress, and now I was there.

I dug my finger into the button, wishing my heart would hamper its rapid beating. I needed to apologize to him first if I was going to seduce him.

"Evelyn?"

I jumped at Ethan's voice behind me. He always called me Evelyn. At first, it bugged me, but I'd grown to like it. His gaze swept over my strappy dress, paused at my breasts, then landed on my face.

He did not appear amused.

Begrudgingly, I noted his undeniable hotness rivaled August in New York City. His aviator glasses concealed his eyes but accentuated his rigid jawline and complemented his chestnut hair, which was swept to the side, adding to his irresistible charm.

His shirt was concealed by the carton of wine in his arms, but his muscular legs fit nice and snug in his dark jeans. All he needed was an aviator jacket and a jet between his thighs and I'd take him right there on the sidewalk.

"Hi." I swallowed.

It hit me that I wasn't just there because I needed Ethan for my ultimate revenge. I'd been unsettled ever since our fight a week ago.

My sleep had been restless, and it wasn't from any spiders (which I'd collected and put back in their container). It was because I didn't like Ethan mad at me.

"What are you doing here?" His voice dripped with annoyance.

Okay, maybe it was a little weird to be outside his apartment when I'd never been there before. It felt very stalkerish.

"Er...I've been trying to get ahold of you." I pulled my lips into a smile, but it felt more like a grimace.

He shifted the carton, the well-knit muscles in his arms flexing under his tan skin at the strain of holding it. Ethan elbowed me aside and looked into a square panel. The door to the building clicked open.

"Did that scan your eye?" I asked, impressed.

"Yeah." He bumped the door with his hip.

"Aren't you afraid a thief is gonna gouge your eye out to break in?"

Ethan stared at me.

"Guess not," I said.

"I'm busy. I'll call you later." Ethan stepped inside, leaving me behind, but I caught the door with the toe of my sandal.

"What are you doing?" Ethan asked, halting in the white-marbled foyer.

"Stop being a dick, Ethan, and invite me upstairs," I said, my irritation eclipsing my attempt to be sweet.

His face darkened, and he didn't budge.

"Look, I just need any photos you have of Joe and me. You've known us as a couple the longest, and any day we'll be getting the appointment for the interview," I said, using the excuse I'd made up to be there. "They want proof of the relationship."

"I'll email you anything I find." He elbowed the elevator button.

I pulled a bottle from the carton and looked at the label. "This is a good one."

He snorted and stepped into the elevator, and I squeezed beside him. He grumbled, but he didn't push me out.

"You know wine?" he asked.

"Nope." I dumped the bottle back into the box and his arms wavered.

The elevator opened directly into his loft. We walked down a short hallway, entering the spacious living area. The apartment boasted an open-plan design, with vaulted ceilings, arched windows spanning the far wall, and a seamless blend of classical architecture and modern stylings. Despite its lavishness, it emitted a cozy and inviting atmosphere.

"I'm sorry, but this is all wrong." I waved my hand around the room. I'd meant it as a joke because what twenty-five-year-old lived like this? Ethan didn't crack a smile.

"Dude, you're meant to be living in a shoebox with five other roommates." I shook my head, dropping my purse on the gray sectional, making it clear I wasn't going anywhere soon. "I feel sorry for you."

Ethan placed the wine on the sleek white-and-gray quartz island in the modern kitchen, revealing the playful teddy bear balloon print on his short-sleeved, button-down shirt.

"Nice shirt," I said.

"Thanks," he said, narrowing his gaze. "Why do you feel sorry for me?"

"You'll never understand the thrill of eating peanut butter and jelly sandwiches every day for dinner and staying warm by opening your oven when the landlord turns down the heat. It's called struggling, and it builds character."

His cheek twitched like he was holding back a smile...or a scowl.

"I'd be happy to switch places with you for a while if you want to have the real New Yorker experience." I shrugged. "It's the least I can do."

He didn't crack a smile. Huh. Maybe it was a bad idea to come here and invade his personal space. He was a private person.

On second thought...

I walked past him and down a wide hallway off the living room.

"Where are you going?" His long strides overtook me, but I was spry and ducked around him, nudging open the double doors to the master bedroom. He rushed past me, knocking my shoulder, and stashed something into his nightstand drawer.

"Was that a butt plug?" I asked with a smirk.

"No," he barked.

"Anal beads?" I tried again.

"Knock it off."

"A tub of KY to rub one out?" I asked. "I keep a few sex toys in my nightstand. Easy access."

His cheeks colored and he went all squirmy. His unease amused me more than I wanted to admit.

"Don't be ashamed." I smiled sweetly. "My favorite is the rose, but it should be illegal. I've never come so hard in—"

"Enough," he said, his fists clenched in front of his pants.

"My neighbors called the police once because I

screamed so loud," I said, a thrill rushing down my spine. This wasn't true, but man, it was fun to tease Ethan.

Ethan groaned, a mix between pleasure and pain.

"Why won't you move your hands, Ethan?" I asked, realizing what he was covering.

"You're evil, Evelyn," he grumbled, the muscles in his neck straining.

I slid my fingers across the drawer, circling the handle, and he spun, snatching my hand away.

"Don't," he warned.

My gaze snapped to his pants and the prominent erection that pressed against his jeans pocket.

I squealed in triumph and pointed. "Ha! I knew it."

Ethan dropped my hand and stood there, making no move to hide the outline of his erection. His eyes locked with mine, and my good mood vanished, replaced with a burning heat that immediately made me feel exposed.

Ethan Steele was a step away with a full-on erection. My breath shortened, and my tongue played with the corner of my mouth as I imagined him dropping trow, exposing what looked like a very impressive cock.

I moaned involuntarily and slammed my hand over my mouth.

"Something wrong, Evelyn?" he asked, crossing his arms.

"No," I peeped.

He didn't move, a challenge in his eyes.

"What are you doing?" I asked, willing myself not to look at his cock, but *damn* it was tempting.

"Waiting," he answered.

I didn't have to ask what he was waiting on.

"O-kay," I elongated the word. "I'll wait too."

Ethan rolled his eyes and walked into the bathroom, clicking the door shut.

I sank onto his crisp, white duvet and rested against his pillows, stretching my legs out in front of me.

"Are you jerking off in there?" I hollered after a couple of minutes passed.

The door flung open, and it hit the doorstopper, vibrating. His gaze raked up and down where I lounged.

"Get out of my bed, Evelyn," he growled.

I bit my lip but didn't move.

"Get the fuck off my bed," he barked, and my nerves jumped. I swung my feet to the floor.

Ethan pressed his hand between my shoulder blades and shoved me out of his room and down the hall, not stopping until we reached the elevator.

"Wait. I wanted to apologize," I said, wiggling away.

"You're doing a really crappy job," he said.

The spaghetti strap of my dress slid down my arm, exposing the top of my breast. I left it there.

"I'm sorry I was a jerk to you last weekend," I said.

I was gonna stop there and leave, but Ethan stared at me with a stone-cold expression.

"What?" I flung my hands in the air exasperated. "Why are you looking at me like that?"

"Like what?" He continued to glare.

"Like you hate me," I breathed out. "I don't get you, Ethan. You act like you can't stand me, and then you get a hard-on. Twice."

"You were talking about sex and lube and orgasms and you were standing there with your tits hanging out of your dress. My cock got hard," he boomed. "It's been a while, okay? I'm only human."

Heat shot up my neck, but I pressed on. "And on the fire escape?"

In the moment, I'd barely registered it, but later, when I thought back, I remembered something long and hard against my hip when Ethan was on top of me, and I'd been stunned when I'd realized what it had been.

"Your hips were writhing against me as you squirmed, and my body reacted. Trust me, it was the last thing I wanted that night." His eyes closed in a long blink. "It wasn't personal, Evelyn."

That stung, but I said, "Try and keep your libido in check next time."

Ethan jammed the button to the elevator and the doors opened.

I stayed put.

"Don't make me drag you out of here," he said, and I didn't doubt that he would.

"Wait," I said, remembering. "The photos."

"I sent them to you while I was in the bathroom."

Remembering my bag, I walked to the sofa and slid my phone out, checking my email for them, but another message caught my attention and I gasped, my hands shaking.

"What?" Ethan was by my side in an instant.

"The interview's been scheduled. It's in two weeks." I swayed sideways, and Ethan grabbed my elbow, lowering me onto the large sectional.

"Isn't that good news?" Ethan asked, sitting next to me on the wide cushion.

I nodded, but my chin quivered. This meant I was one step closer to getting my citizenship, and once that happened, my marriage would officially be dead.

The plotting and scheming had been a great distraction, and I was eager to get more revenge on the fucker, but once that was done, what would happen?

There'd be no more Joe. No marriage. No more perfect future. Where would I live? Would I find someone I could trust enough to marry again and start a family?

Sure, I could have kids on my own, but I didn't want to. I wanted to have a partner by my side, and I'd thought that partner was Joe.

I fell forward, and my hands gripped the coffee table as I sucked air into my constricted lungs. Sobs threatened, and my throat ached from holding them down.

"Evelyn, are you okay?" Ethan's alarmed voice rang out beside me.

I ran into the guest bathroom, snatched the hand

towel, and sank to the floor, shoving it in my mouth as I broke into heaving sobs.

I was vaguely aware of Ethan behind me, his hand resting on my back, letting me know he was there.

When I was able to suck deep breaths into my lungs, I rocked back on my heels, embarrassed by the outburst. I kept the towel to my face, my back to Ethan, who sat quietly beside me, his hand still on my bare shoulder blade.

"I hate him," I spoke roughly into the towel, my voice sticky from the tears. "I fucking hate him."

"I know." Ethan dropped his hand but stayed on the floor next to me.

"The anger consumes me." I hiccupped over a whimper. "I want him to be in as much agony as me."

I threw the towel on the counter and splashed cold water on my face, clearing the fog. Ethan hovered behind me, and I studied him in the mirror.

"You can be a real ass, you know that?" I said, shaking my head. "But when I'm in pain, you become this different person. Do you have some sort of injured animal complex?"

Ethan's jaw worked under his skin like he was debating how to respond. Unlike me, Ethan wasn't reactive. His emotions were controlled and calculated. It was impossible to know what was going on in his head because he masked it before it was revealed.

He was saved from answering by the buzz of his intercom.

Ethan walked to the entryway, and I followed him.

He stared at the image on the small video screen on the wall but made no move to speak to the person or buzz them up.

"Who is it?" I asked.

Ethan turned to me, a shadow curtaining his features.

"Joe."

# Chapter 12

## *Ethan*

The intercom buzzed again. I glanced at Eva, her eyes wide like a deer that had stepped in line with a hunter's rifle and knew its fate.

There was a stab in my chest at her distress. I ignored it, but after her panic attack in the bathroom, it wasn't easy.

Dammit, she was right. Something happened to me when she was suffering. It was like the chemicals in my body changed and my instinct was to fiercely protect her.

"Don't let him up," she said, her voice shaking.

I was about to assure her I wasn't an idiot when the elevator hummed and began its descent to the ground floor. I clicked the video screen and switched it to the camera in the lobby.

"He's in the lobby waiting for the elevator," I told Eva. My shoulders tensed, worried she was going to freak out again.

"What the hell, Ethan?" She slammed her fist into my right pectoral, and dull pain shot into my muscle. "Why did you let him in?"

She wound up for another strike and I stepped sideways. She was small, but she packed a solid punch.

"I didn't buzz him up," I grunted.

How the hell did I get into this mess with her?

"I forgot he was coming over tonight." I frowned at the screen. Her sudden arrival at my apartment had fried my brain and it slipped my mind. "He has the entry code."

Her eyebrows rose, but we didn't have time to discuss it. Through the video com, the elevator chimed, indicating its arrival in the lobby. Joe stepped inside.

"He'll be here in sixty seconds," I said.

Evelyn glared at me like this was my fault, and I sliced my gaze back at her.

"I didn't invite you up here, sweetheart," I ground out. "You pushed your way in and wouldn't leave."

She'd always been determined, but ever since I found her falling apart in the bridal suite, she'd become a strange, unhinged creature. It was like a beautiful train wreck I couldn't take my eyes off of.

I tugged her elbow toward the coat closet.

"Get in here."

Her eyes were alight with turmoil, but she let me pull her inside, reality sinking in. Even if we could think up a good lie as to why she was here, Joe would be suspicious. He knew we barely tolerated each other.

Fury radiated from her, but she sank backward, the coats eclipsing her.

I couldn't imagine the hell she was going through living with a man who was sleeping with another woman. If it had been me and I had to pretend all was right as fucking rain, there'd be a lot of bloody punching bags and late-night drinking.

The elevator opened as I clicked the door shut on Eva.

"What the hell, man?" Joe said, but he was smiling, and he grabbed my hand, squeezing it between us as he patted my back in a quick hug. "Didn't you hear me buzzing?"

"I was on the phone." I lifted it up for good measure.

Joe went to the kitchen and popped a beer open. He offered me one, but I declined. I wasn't sure I could control myself if I drank right now.

Joe strutted around my place, his chest puffed out. This was a defensive stance. After two decades, I'd become familiar with Joe's differing moods. I used to overlook his jealous streaks and narcissistic tendencies, but I could barely keep the bile down when I witnessed it these days.

Part of me wanted to beat the shit out of him, but I held back for Eva's sake. I wasn't going to screw up her citizenship, plus it had been deeply satisfying watching Joe squirm over the past few weeks with the little revenge games that we played on him.

"I should be the one living like a king, man." Joe

swung his arms wide around my living room. He laughed like he was joking, but I knew he meant it. Our friendship worked best when Joe was on top. The moment it flipped, he became a dick.

"I'm gonna tell you something, but don't get all self-righteous and shit, okay?" Joe sat on the edge of my distressed leather armchair. "I'm gonna break up with Eva."

In the hallway closet, there was a loud bump. Joe was studying my reaction and didn't notice.

"What the hell, man?" I raked my hand through my hair, stunned. "You just got married."

"Hey, there's a lot of shit going on that you don't know about." Joe choked the neck of his beer. "You were right. She doesn't love me. All she cares about is her citizenship and her new hip job in the city and whatever the next step on her goal chart is."

He stood up, then sat down, then stood up again and paced the room.

"I noticed it a couple of months before the big cere- mony. But we were already married, and I didn't want to disappoint Tiffany and Luis. It would've killed them," Joe said, referring to his parents, who adored Eva. "Did you know we haven't had sex in four months? Fuck." He shook his head in disbelief.

For a moment, I saw the six-year-old boy I'd first met, bloodied from being pushed off his skateboard by some older kid. Joe had acted tough, but he was in pain.

I'd walked home with him. I didn't say anything,

just stayed by his side in solidarity. The worst thing he could've done was show weakness in front of the older kids, but I knew he was humiliated.

We didn't say a word that afternoon, but the next day he waited for me after school, and we rode down to the skate park together. After that, we were inseparable.

"Have you talked to Evelyn about this?" I asked.

"What's the point? She'd just add *sex with Joe* to her to-do list. How messed up is that? I don't want sex to be scheduled for the rest of my life. I want passion, man. You know?"

I ground my jaw and said calmly, "Yeah, man. I totally get it."

Joe exhaled and gulped his beer until it was done, then went to the fridge and got another.

"It's like you said. She has a hole where her heart should be." He sat down and placed the beer on the coffee table, running his hands over his thighs.

Blood drained from my face. I'd forgotten I said that. It had been when I was feeling particularly sorry for myself over Jasmin.

*Fuck.* I prayed Eva hadn't heard Joe.

"There's something else," Joe said.

My muscles tensed, sensing what he was about to confess.

"I got back with Ashley."

"Holy shit," I said in faux shock. "How long? And what do you mean *got back*?"

"A few...weeks," Joe said. A lie. "I didn't mean for it

to happen, but I've got blue balls here. It's not right. I'm a newlywed and I haven't even fucked my wife."

Joe swallowed, his gaze locked on me, waiting for my judgment. I schooled my features, not showing anything but surprise and confusion, but my hands were fisted behind my back as I held back my anger. I wanted to grab him by the collar and tell him this was not how you treat your wife. This wasn't how you treat any woman.

"You can't tell her," I said, refocusing on the most important thing. "Her citizenship interview should be coming any day, right? Don't mess that up for her."

Joe cocked his head, studying me. "Why do you care? You've wanted me to leave her from the day we started dating. You said she's worthless."

"I never said that," I snapped. "I mean, yeah, I care about you, man, and I agree. I didn't think she was as into you as you were into her. But you told me to fuck off and you married her anyway. Don't screw up her new job. Wait a few more weeks."

Joe rolled his eyes, and I realized he'd already made up his mind. "Nah. I can't do it. It's not fair to keep lying to her."

"Bullshit," I said, my anger slipping out. "You just want it to be easier for you. If she doesn't get her citizenship, she can't stay in the country, and then you won't have to deal with your mess." I punched the arm of the sofa. "You've done some selfish shit, Joe, but this is beyond. Just man up and wait. You don't need to ruin her life."

Joe shot to standing, his face beet red. "She ruined *my* life! She used me for her green card. I know it. She doesn't love me. You were right all along. Why are you all defensive?"

I heard shuffling from the closet and glanced toward it, but then snapped my gaze back to Joe. I hated that she had to hear all this, but I was also glad. She needed to know exactly what Joe was capable of.

"I'm not," I said. "But don't be cruel. Even if she doesn't love you, none of it was malicious. Like you said, she goes through life with a checklist, and she probably got so focused on the wedding she never asked herself if this was what she really wanted."

"What, me?" Joe scoffed.

"All of it," I said, but Joe wasn't going to change his mind. He'd come here because he thought he'd have an ally since I'd been against Eva and him at the beginning.

"It's too late. I'm telling her tonight." He chucked his beer bottle in the sink and charged for the door. "Be my best friend and get behind this."

The elevator doors sat open, and Joe stepped inside and jammed his finger on the button panel, the doors sliding shut.

There was a hush in the entryway after Joe left. I took a moment to tamp down my heart rate, then I walked to the closet.

"He's gone," I said.

When Eva opened the door, I expected her to either be in tears or in a rage. She was neither. Her hands were clasped tightly in front of her, but she was strangely calm.

"Are you okay?" I cupped her elbow, and she flinched as if my fingers were a lit match.

"Never better." She smiled tightly, fixed her purse strap on her shoulder, and walked to the elevator but didn't press the button. She just stood there.

"What are you doing?" I asked, unnerved by her cool composure.

"Waiting to make sure Joe is gone before I leave."

I shoved my hands in my jeans pockets. "Come on, Evelyn, give me some shit. Tell me I'm an asshole. Tell me Joe's an asshole. I know you heard everything."

She slid her steely gaze to me. Yep. She definitely heard everything.

"What are you going to do?" I asked, almost desperate to get some kind of reaction out of her. "Joe wants a divorce."

"I'm not worried." She smiled contemptuously. "You obviously don't know how to control him. But I do."

She elbowed the button, and a moment later the door opened. She stepped inside and held the door ajar with her hand.

"He's not going to break up with me. And we"—she pointed her finger between us—"are going to start the next phase of the revenge pact."

I furrowed my brow, trying to remember if we'd discussed another scheme.

With the fingers of her left hand, she tugged the

scoop neck of her dress down, exposing the dark, half-moon tops of her areoles.

She leaned forward and whispered, "Let's give him a taste of his own medicine."

"What?" I blinked rapidly, a rush of desire filling my cock to engorgement.

She dipped forward and her fingers dusted across my jeans where my dick pressed against the material.

"I think *he* understands my meaning."

She stepped inside the waiting elevator and adjusted her dress, the lust on her face dropping, replaced by a sweet smile.

"Have a good day."

Blood pumped behind my ears, whirring along with the sound of the disappearing elevator.

"Oh fuck," I said to the empty entryway as her full meaning crashed into my gut.

She wanted a revenge affair. With me.

I'd seen it on her revenge board, but I didn't think she'd do it.

Not with me.

My jaw clenched as the images of the naked mounds of her breasts seared my brain, and my cock overheated.

No. I couldn't do it. It was a line too far.

I'd go to my room. Pull out the lube I'd flung in my drawer, pump my cock until I howled, and forget I'd ever met Evelyn Hart.

# Chapter 13

## *Eva*

"I kinda like this new you." Rachel sat at the edge of the long table where I was finishing an email.

Dreamary occupied a whole floor in the squat, modern building in Chelsea. The space was designed with clean lines and an open-plan layout, featuring workbenches instead of cubicles, a spattering of offices for the executives, and two recording studios. The aim of the design was to create a more fluid and equal atmosphere, without any sense of hierarchy.

Or something like that.

I liked it because the space was stylish and warm with lots of green plants and dark wood accents. There was a platform at one end with pillows and beanbag chairs where you could hang out or meditate or take a yoga class when offered.

"What do you mean?" I asked, pushing my rolling chair back. It was late afternoon on Tuesday, four days since I'd overheard Joe telling Ethan that he was planning to dump me.

Wait. Not dump me. Divorce me.

I shook my head internally. Twenty-four was too young to be divorced. Not even Ross had his first divorce by then. (I'd recently discovered *Friends* and binged the first six seasons.)

"You're a little manic," Rachel said.

I wrinkled my nose. "That doesn't sound good."

"We all need to go a little mad sometimes." Rachel picked at the large, white Band-Aid on her shoulder. She'd been slammed against the arena wall during her last roller derby tournament and her shoulder got the brunt of the injury.

Derrick, one of the co-owners of Dreamary, walked down the wide aisle toward me. He'd started the company three years ago with his friend and colleague Isaac Pillon after Isaac and Derrick's podcast *Missing Girls* exploded. Isaac was a true crime journalist, and they were both major activists in solving missing cases, especially those involving minority women.

Rachel swept her gaze over his tall frame. He was an ex-detective, with a hardened demeanor but a kind heart. Isaac and he had been a big reason why I'd fought so hard for this job.

I'd been on a mission to secure a job before I graduated college and attended every business lecture and seminar that came through Syracuse. Not the university but the city. I created a chart with the dates and venues and the companies represented.

I researched the speakers and wrote down two or three questions and an interesting fact that I could bring up. After each talk, I waited, sometimes hours, to meet the speaker and begin a dialogue I hoped to turn into an interview if I liked the company.

Half the time the speaker smiled politely and gave me their card, but nothing ever came of it.

Dreamary had been top of my list from the moment I heard Derrick and Isaac speak about diversity and vulnerability in the workplace.

Ultimately, my goal was to work with a foundation to fund diverse programs in local communities. Everything Derrick and his company did was in line with my beliefs. It wasn't a direct trajectory to managing a foundation, but because of their work and the leaders they interviewed in their different podcast programs, there were tons of opportunities to network and get a foot into the world of philanthropy.

When I approached Derrick after his talk, we started an exchange through email, and after a month he invited me in for an interview. I went and they hired me.

"Alexis just called," Derrick said, stopping in front of my chair. "Her producer, Fatima, can't come in tomorrow. Her child's sick with strep. Can you fill in as producer? It's just for some intros. No interviews."

Rachel stared at Derrick like he was an oasis of water after a month in the desert. I elbowed her in the ribs, and she sat back with an unapologetic shrug.

Derrick was a good-looking man, but he was forty-five and my boss, so very off-limits.

Not to mention I was married and about to start an affair with my husband's best friend.

"Absolutely. Is Fatima still here?" I asked.

"Yes. Her husband's with their daughter, but she's leaving after she finishes a pre-interview with a guest for next week. She'll send you what you need later today so you can prep for tomorrow."

"Perfect." I smiled, and Derrick walked away.

Rachel melted off her chair to the floor, her hand to her chest as if she was overcome by Derrick's handsomeness.

"You should have your revenge affair with him," Rachel said, blowing a strand of pink hair out of her face.

"It's gonna be challenging enough having an affair. I'm not bringing that mess into work. This is my sanctuary. I'd go insane without it."

Ethan had texted me several times after I left, but I'd ignored him. Not because I wasn't ready to follow through—I was determined to give Joe the same punch in the guts he gave me on our wedding day—but first I had to stop Joe from ending us too soon.

He was on his way to my office now.

"Do you want to go over the questions while we wait?" Rachel pulled up the one hundred questions I could be asked on my citizenship exam. They'd only ask me ten, but I wouldn't know which ten of the hundred.

"I'm not sure I can concentrate right now," I said. "But the lounge is quiet."

In the company lounge, there was a plush sofa, two relaxing hammock chairs, a few cozy armchairs, a compact kitchen, a coffee station, and a wet bar that served draft beer. I took the sofa while Rachel settled on one of the swinging chairs next to me.

We went through several questions, but my focus was scattered, and Rachel eventually gave up.

"I'm sorry. Joe's gonna be here any minute." My heart thumped in my chest, anticipating our plan.

I'd been saved from dodging Joe all weekend because he was called away Friday afternoon on a work emergency at the site that lasted until late last night.

Joe texted this morning and asked me to meet him for happy hour after work, but I told him to meet me here instead to avoid a public scene and because I needed Rachel for my plan to work.

Rachel often stopped by my office after she was done with her shift, so it wouldn't be strange for her to be hanging out here with me when Joe came by. She managed a Pilates studio five blocks away.

"Don't worry. This is gonna work," Rachel said. She leaned forward and squeezed my hand reassuringly, but I was shaking.

If Joe didn't take the bait, then this job was over. My life in New York City was over. Everything I'd built over the past six years was gone.

"Is this my fault?" I asked, deflated. "Joe said I scheduled sex, and he's right. Before the wedding, that's exactly what I would've done. And Ethan told Joe there's a hole where my heart should be. Am I broken?"

"No!" Rachel exploded. "You're a beautiful human with a big heart. It's not your fault your dad messed you up. You just feel safer with an orderly life. Anyone who loves you understands."

"I feel sick." I gripped my stomach. "The room is spinning."

Rachel snapped her fingers in front of my face. "Take deep breaths. It's gonna be fine."

A text pinged my phone and I read it. "He's here."

"Oh shit." Rachel's back stiffened despite her earlier reassurance.

Joe sauntered in, a lazy grin on his face, but there was tension around his eyes. He knew if he broke up with me, I wouldn't just walk away. I'd have lots of questions about why he was suddenly ending us. In his mind, he was breaking my heart (or the gaping hole).

Little did he know he'd crushed it on our wedding day.

"Hey," I said, patting the cushion next to me.

He sat, casually draping his hand over my knee, and I forced my muscles to relax under his touch.

"Rachel popped by to tell me some hot goss." I caught her eye. The plan was in motion.

"I thought we were going to grab a drink," Joe said. "I wanted to talk to you."

"We will." I rubbed his hand. "In a few minutes."

Joe shrugged, as if waiting a few more minutes to

tear our relationship apart was no biggie. He slid his phone out and began scrolling.

"Is the guy married?" I asked Rachel as if we'd been in the middle of a conversation.

"Not sure," Rachel said. "All Ashley said was her new guy was cheating on his girl to be with her."

Joe's phone crashed to the floor.

Rachel and I glanced at him sideways but pretended we didn't notice the slight shake in his hand when he picked up the phone.

"Ashley told you—" Joe stopped abruptly. "I mean, what are you talking about? What's this gossip?"

"Oh, just the same Ashley bullshit." Rachel waved her hand as if Ashley always had drama. Which she did. "She's all excited about some guy she stole away from his girlfriend or whatever. She thinks he's gonna leave the poor girl for her. If you ask me, everyone in this scenario is a schmuck."

Joe tensed next to me. "Maybe she really likes the guy and he realized he made a mistake with his girlfriend."

I swung a confused gaze at him. "Why are you defending her?"

"I'm not. Never mind. I don't care." Joe leaned back and stared at his phone, but he was stiff as a board.

"Oh, I'm sure Ashley thinks she loves this guy," Rachel continued, turning toward me and leaning forward, her elbows on her knees. "But she'll lose interest the moment the guy leaves his girlfriend. She loves winning. That's the exciting part, but once she gets the prize, suddenly Mr. Amazing becomes Mr. Boring. What's exciting about a guy that's available?"

"Wow." I sat back as if thinking. "Would she go to all that trouble? You said she knows the guy's girlfriend, right?"

"Are you kidding?" Rachel snorted. Joe's hand gripped his phone so tight that his knuckles were white. "She does this every time. She chases after an ungetatable guy, nails him, and suddenly her infatuation is over and she's done with the guy. This is no different."

"You don't know that," Joe snapped.

Rachel patted Joe's shoulder patronizingly. "I'm sorry, but do you have amnesia? Remember that English TA Ashley chased during her sophomore year? She was practically obsessed with him. She finally slept with him, and a week later she forgot his name."

"And that single dad that worked at the vet office she interned at one summer," I said.

Joe shoved his phone into his pocket, his attention fully on the conversation.

"Don't you remember, babe?" I asked.

"Er, yeah," he said, shifting on the sofa.

"He had no interest in her, but she wouldn't stop pursuing him until he finally took her out. A month later, the program ended and she never mentioned him again. She got what she wanted."

Rachel nodded. "Ashley's my friend. I don't mean to be harsh. But *gawd*. How many times does the girl have to prove she can get the man? I know she doesn't realize she's doing it. When she's pursuing these guys, she really believes she likes them."

Joe's jaw was grinding under his tawny skin, his gaze darkening.

"It might be different this time," Joe said. "Ashley wasn't like that when we dated."

My throat constricted, and I held in a whimper. Joe barely talked about when they went out.

"Yeah, she was." Rachel raised her eyebrows like *duh*. "She met you when you were heartbroken over Keisha. Ashley said you were barely into the relationship with her at first. Eventually, you two fell in love, and it was good for a bit. But..." Rachel hesitated, her tone gentle. "Wasn't it Ashley who broke up with you?"

Joe fisted his hands in his lap. "It was mutual."

"Anyways." Rachel waved her hand, moving on. "If this guy really does dump his girlfriend, he's gonna be left holding his dick without a pussy."

"You're so fucking crude, Rachel," Joe snapped.

Rachel threw her hands up in a half apology but smirked. "Just saying it like it is. Even she'd admit she loves the chase more than the relationship."

"Did she say anything else about the guy?"

"Not really," Rachel said, relaxing back against the chair. "She asked me not to say anything, but seeing as she's fucking some woman's boyfriend, I don't feel bad speaking about her totally immoral relationship. Plus, I trust you guys. And you both know Ashley. You know what she's like."

"I have to go." Joe stood and yanked his phone out of his pocket.

The air constricted in my chest. Had we done it? Had we convinced Joe that breaking up with me meant Ashley would break up with him?

"But I thought we were going out." I dropped my voice into a whine.

He pecked me on the cheek. "Sorry, babe. Work just messaged. There are still issues with that pipe that burst. Don't wait up."

I dropped to the sofa, my knees shaking. Rachel slid next to me and put her arms around my shoulders. I bent my head and began crying.

Joe was on his way to Ashley. I doubted he'd say anything about this conversation. He'd be determined to make sure she loved him and would stay with him.

I couldn't get the image of him running to her and away from me out of my head.

"He doesn't deserve you," Rachel said.

"Of course he doesn't," I spat out. "He deserves to be crushed like a bug. He hates me. He's about to spend the night with her. Did you hear him? *Don't wait up.*"

I stormed out of the lounge. It was just after six. I typically stayed late on Mondays to get my schedule in order for the week, but I couldn't concentrate when another part of my life was falling apart.

"I don't want to feel like this," I said, charging for the elevator.

"Like what?" Rachel asked, jogging to keep up.

"Unhinged!" I jammed my finger into the button. "Tonight begins a new game. A game that I control."

# Chapter 14

## *Ethan*

My phone lit up with my front door camera, and Eva's face filled the screen. Her brow was furrowed, and her lips pressed together tightly, but she wrung her hands, betraying her nervousness.

I'd debated contacting her all week to tell her to forget the pact, forget the insane idea of an affair, but something stopped me from sending the text.

Eva's life was in a tailspin. I understood. I'd lost my best friend since childhood. That hurt in a way I wasn't ready to claim.

I buzzed her up. Oh hell, this was a bad idea.

The elevator doors opened, and I opened my mouth to tell her calmly that we should talk, but Eva jumped on me. The little sprite pounced on me, her legs wrapping around my waist. Instinctively, my hands grabbed under her thighs, and we slammed into the wall. Her mouth crashed into mine, our teeth clashing painfully.

"Whoa," I said, pushing back. Her mouth searched for mine, but I peeled her supple limbs from me until her feet touched the ground.

"What was that?" I asked, running my finger across my front teeth soothingly.

The air crackled with her anger, fire alighting her eyes.

"I want to destroy him," she fumed.

"Come here, crazy." I took her hand and pulled her to the kitchen, settling her onto a stool.

I spun the cap off a glass water bottle and placed it on the counter in front of her. She raised her eyebrow, the message clear—she wanted something stronger.

I found Tito's in the freezer and poured it into a glass with orange juice. She drank a big gulp and then leveled her gaze at me.

"What's the problem?" she asked, bitterness on her tongue.

"You're a little scary right now," I said honestly.

She shrugged. "Let's use that energy. Get a little wild."

She sucked down more of her drink. Her words were strong, but there was a tremble in her voice.

"I know you want me." She smiled coyly. "Your dick was hard for me the last time I was here."

I choked on a cough.

"Fuck, Evelyn. Can we forget that? There were a few things going on that afternoon."

She crossed her arms. "Like what?"

"Like I'd been planning to jerk off before you came over."

Eva frowned like she didn't believe me. "Were you going to rub one out on the street?"

"I was about to take care of business when the wine shop called and said my order was ready and they were about to close. So I ran out." I couldn't believe I was telling her this.

"That was KY on your nightstand, wasn't it?" she asked.

I nodded. I'd been all riled up, ready to choke the sausage, when I'd run downstairs. The shop was two doors away. Then she showed up looking like sex on a summer day, batting her eyes, teasing me about sex toys and anal and showing me her tits.

"I know you're not my biggest fan, but there's obviously *something* you like about me. Physically, at least." The undercurrent of vulnerability in her tone squeezed at my heart.

Joe had never really known Eva. Not her soft parts, the ones she kept hidden. I was certain of that now.

When I found her in the bridal suite, broken apart from his deception, I felt like a complete ass. Maybe she hadn't let Joe into her heart, but she'd loved him in her way. And ever since then, I hadn't been able to look her in the eyes without feeling a stab of guilt.

"So it could've been anybody standing in front of you. You were just horny?" she asked, back to the whole        you-were-about-to-masturbate-and-then-I-showed-up thing.

I flashed my gaze at her, but I couldn't tell if she was manipulating me in that subtle way I'd noticed she was good at or not.

"I told you, your body in that dress did that to me." Then I quickly added, "I'm not blaming you. I'm just saying. You looked fucking hot, Evelyn."

She smiled. "So you want me for my body?"

"I never said I wanted you," I grumbled. "I hate Joe, but fucking his girl takes this to a whole other level. There's no coming back if we cross this line," I said honestly.

"He fucked the love of your life and he's currently cheating on me. The line's been obliterated."

I exhaled, my chest tightening as we took one step closer to doing this.

"We'll need ground rules," I said. "*If* I agree to this."

Her face beamed. "Now you're talking my language."

"I don't want us to get confused. This can't be sex like we'd have in a normal relationship." Fuck, I couldn't believe I was talking about having sex with Eva.

"How do you mean?"

"We could role-play?" I suggested.

"Like secretary and boss?" she asked.

"Maybe."

"I get to be the boss!" She put her hand up like she was in class.

"Do you have a fantasy?" I asked, warming to this idea.

It was one thing to sleep with Joe's girl; it was another to risk having real feelings for her. This could get complicated fast. Role-playing would add a layer of distance.

Eva pressed her palms into the quartz countertop, considering. "I don't know. Sex has always been mechanical, not fantastical."

This bothered me more than I'd expected, and it meant one thing.

"You've never had great sex," I said.

Her cheeks bloomed pink, and I quickly added, "I'm not blaming you." I rubbed my brow. "I hate to ask this, but how was sex with Joe?"

"Bland, but relationships aren't just about that."

There was a tug in my chest. "For people who are asexual. Is that you?" I held my breath, suddenly terrified by what she was gonna say next.

"Um, I don't think so. Sex can be good. Like finally scratching a mosquito bite that's hard to reach."

I rolled my eyes.

"Let's go back to my earlier question. Have you ever had a fantasy?" I asked. Her pink cheeks darkened, guilt covering her features. "You do have a fantasy."

She dropped her gaze. "A guy taking complete control, almost forcing himself on me. With my total consent, of course. I'd have to really trust him. But I think I'd...um, like it."

My mind filled with a vision of me pinning her down and taking her against the kitchen counter where she hovered.

I cleared my throat, trying to keep the heat out of my voice. "That makes sense. Your life's regimented. It would probably be nice to let go and let someone else take the reins for a while."

"Do you have a fantasy?" she asked. "I'd rather do yours first."

"My life is a fantasy."

I meant it. For a guy who grew up in a fucked-up household with little stability, having more money than I ever imagined before I was thirty was a dream. But I knew this wasn't what she was asking.

"Do you like butt stuff? To be dominated? Submissive? Furries? Cosplay? Voyeurism?"

I bit the inside of my cheek and held back a laugh. "Did you say furries?"

Her eyes widened. "Is that your fetish?"

I shook my head. "No. I like skin-to-skin contact. That would be too much...material."

"Come on, Ethan." She exhaled loudly, her brownish-green eyes narrowing. "What do you want to do? We don't have to role-play. We can just fuck."

And with that, she pulled her top off.

I swallowed over the lust pressing into my throat. God, I knew her tits were pretty, but to see them fully was amazing. Small and perky. Just big enough to fit into my palm, her areoles dark and large, the way I loved them.

"Cosplay," I said, my voice catching. "That's what I like." Saliva filled my mouth, my tongue tingling to lick one of her hardening nipples.

Her mouth hitched up on one side. "Do you have the costumes?"

I shook my head. Several freckles were sprinkled over her right breast, and I wanted to trace the lines between them.

It felt like ice water ran down my back when she pulled her shirt back on.

"Let's go," she said and walked to the elevator, pressing the button.

It took me several seconds to register that she was leaving. I couldn't move, my legs weak after the shock of seeing Eva's breasts. It was wrong, but everything in me wanted it to be right.

"Where are you going?" I asked, panicked.

"*We're* going to pick out costumes. I'm fine if you need me to be someone else in order to put your dick inside me. At this point, I don't care."

It wasn't that I wanted her to be someone else. I wanted her not to be Joe's girl. I wanted to get lost in her and not have that niggling voice telling me that no matter what Joe did to us, this wasn't exactly a great idea.

"We don't need to buy costumes," I said, recovering. "I grew up watching *Law & Order: SVU*. My first sexual fantasies were about Olivia Benson."

Eva's eyes sparkled with excitement.

"Did you have a thing for Stabler?" I asked, hoping that's what I was reading in her heated gaze.

"For both of them." She nibbled her bottom lip, looking into the distance as if she was lost in thought. "She was tough, but her heart bled for those victims."

She pulled out her phone and began making a list. "I'll need a suit. And a badge and handcuffs. Wait, what are you going to be? A perp? Stabler?"

My heart was pounding, excited about the possibilities. "You're wearing black slacks," I said, suddenly not wanting to delay this. "I have a white, button-down shirt that shrunk in the wash. Put that on. And—"

"I'll make it work. What about the cuffs?" she asked, charging toward my bedroom.

"Wait," I said. "I have a cop outfit from an old college party. It has a badge and a pair of handcuffs."

In the back of my closet, I found the button-down shirt and gave it to her before I had the sense to stop this runaway train. She went in the bathroom to change and *freshen up*—whatever that meant—and I went to the office and rummaged through an old box of clothes.

At the bottom I found the police outfit and pulled out the items, placing them beside me on the rug. I was bent over the box, searching for the baton, when my arm was twisted behind me roughly. I lost my balance and fell sideways as Eva jammed her knee in my back and yanked my arm further up my spine.

I yelped.

"Shut up." Using her body weight, she pressed my face into the navy shag rug. The starched collar of her shirt rubbed against the back of my neck. "Don't move, scumbag."

I squirmed because my shoulder hurt, but I was impressed by her skills. She'd obviously had some sort of fight training.

"Get off me," I grunted and yanked my arm. She let go immediately.

I glanced behind me, confused. She'd tucked the white button-down into her pants, the first two buttons open, her breasts peeking out. Somehow she'd folded her long, blonde hair under so it looked like a bob. She'd snatched the handcuffs from the floor, and they were hanging from one of the belt loops.

Damn, she looked fucking amazing, and in a rush, blood pumped into my cock.

"Why did you stop?" I asked.

"You told me to."

"I was playing along."

"Oh. Should we have a safe word?"

"Stop."

She laughed and nodded, and before I could say another word, she flung her weight on me, snatched my right arm up my back again, and dug her knee into my kidney.

"You have the right to keep your mouth shut." I heard metal clank, and she tugged my other arm behind me and clicked on the handcuffs.

They were cheap, and I'm pretty sure I could get

out of them if I had to, but it felt damn vulnerable to have my arms locked behind my back.

Her hips lowered against my ass, her chest flush with my back. Her breath was hot on my neck as her lips grazed my lobe.

"You're my bitch now," she whispered.

My cock swelled to full engorgement. It ached inside my pants, begging to be set free and manhandled by this dominant version of Eva.

Maybe this wasn't a bad idea. Maybe this was the best fucking idea I'd ever had.

# Chapter 15

## *Eva*

A thrill raced down my back as I pressed Ethan's face to the ground in front of the desk in his home office. My knee jabbed into his back, creating enough pressure against his kidney to make him comply.

He twisted beneath me like he wanted to take back control, but I think he was surprised to discover I had him in a secure hold I'd learned at a self-defense class during high school. I made sure to brush up yearly.

Luckily, I'd never had to use it IRL, but it was thrilling to know this maneuver worked. At least in this role-playing scenario.

I wasn't as nervous as I'd normally be in a new sexual situation. The only explanation was that this impromptu cosplay had turned me into someone else. It helped that I'd been parroting lines from Benson on SVU. Confidence raced through me like a river.

Typically, I lay back and let the guy do his business

as I counted down the minutes until I could roll over and read.

This felt different. My sex pulsed like it was parched and the only thing that could sate it was Ethan.

"Spread your knees." I yanked Ethan up by the cuffs until he was kneeling, his thighs spread wide into a triangle. His back hit my chest, and my breasts flattened against the flexed muscles between his shoulder blades. The fabric of my shirt brushed my nipples, and they tightened into firm nubs.

Slowly, I slid down his back until I found the bottom hem of his shirt. I bit it with my teeth and scraped the material upward to his neck, goose bumps popping up over his naked back.

"Take it off," I said. Staring at cartoon teddy bears wasn't exactly an aphrodisiac.

I unhooked the handcuffs. Ethan yanked the shirt from his head and flipped around, pinning my arms above my head as he pressed me down until I was splayed on the floor. He swung his leg over my hips and straddled my outstretched body.

The corner of his mouth twitched, and he lowered himself inch by inch until he lay on top of me, similar to when we'd been on the fire escape, but this time we were rigid for a different reason.

My breasts tingled, swollen and aching to be touched, as I rocked upward and rubbed against his cock, thick and strained against his pants.

A groan rumbled in his chest and his light eyes

hovered above mine. Silent thoughts bounced between us—Joe...Ethan's initial disdain for me...my mutual loathing...the strangeness of this moment...something softer and unspoken.

This wasn't us. We hated each other.

Except, maybe we didn't.

A wave of self-doubt collided with my confidence and fought until it won, taking away all my courage.

"Stop." I scooted up and pushed my heels into the rug, getting away from him.

Oh God. What was I doing here?

My heart thundered, and I wanted to crawl around the desk and hide. Instead, I dragged my knees up and buried my face.

"Evelyn, look at me." Ethan's voice was strong and demanding.

I flicked my chin up, and my breath was snatched from my lungs. His face held such reverence.

"You're safe. You're sexy as hell. And anything we do or don't do right now will be perfect."

Tears filled my eyes, but I blinked them back, his words pummeling my insecurities out of my mind. I shook my head roughly and asked myself: *What would Benson do?*

"We're not done, shithead." I smiled wryly. "Get back on your knees."

"No," he growled, a glint in his eyes, back in the game. "You've been a bad girl but I'm gonna show you how good it can be."

He wrapped his arms around my ribs and yanked me against his chest, lowering his lips to mine.

I gasped. An electric bolt zipped through me when his mouth touched mine.

My nerves leaped with giddiness, and for a few delicious minutes, it was only this kiss. The soft pads of Ethan's mouth explored my lips, his tongue grazing the seam of my lips. My belly felt nauseous and excited all at once.

How was I kissing Ethan Steele? And how did it feel so fucking amazing? His tongue slid into my mouth, full and ripe, and I sighed.

I banged my hips against his pelvis, my panties sopping beneath my slacks. His hand slid inside the opening of my shirt and cupped my left breast, his fingers rolling my nipple between his thumb and index finger, and I moaned in his mouth, arching my back for more. Jesus, I wanted so much more of this man.

It was surreal and wonderful and strange. Ethan Steele was touching my boob.

His hand continued his exploration, and my heart rate picked up, excitement spun with trepidation.

I'd lost the control I had at the beginning. He was leading, and it felt real. It felt like Ethan and Eva. Not Benson and whomever he was meant to be. The fantasy was dying, and I was frightened of the verity.

"I like being on top," I purred, and as I'd hoped, Ethan complied and rolled to his back. I clambered on top of him, intent on continuing the role-play and escaping the feelings bubbling deep inside me.

My right hand skimmed my hip until it felt cold metal. I flicked the handcuffs open, quickly grabbed Ethan's left hand, and snapped the cuff on. He yelped, but before he could comprehend what I was doing, I wrapped the chain of the cuff around the leg of the desk, then snatched his other hand and secured it too.

His eyes widened with surprise, but excitement skipped over his features.

"I'm in charge of this interrogation," I stated.

His blue eyes sparkled, and a soft, fuzzy feeling entered my chest as we looked at each other.

I tore my gaze away. We weren't here to get close; we were here to get back at Joe and to release our fury at being betrayed.

It was my turn to fuck Joe over.

I ran my hands down the peaks and valleys of Ethan's lean chest. He obviously worked out, but he wasn't overly muscular like Joe. I bent over his smooth, muscled chest and flattened my tongue, licking down his ribbed abdomen.

I wasn't an experienced lover, but I had a strategy. Okay, I may have googled *how to be a good lover* and stuffed pillowcases into some of Joe's clothes and pretended they were Ethan and practiced certain moves on a cucumber and two plums.

The main tip I'd taken away from the articles was to indulge in every part of Ethan and listen to his grunts and moans and do more of what he responded to.

I nipped the skin beneath his belly button with my

teeth, and my finger traced the line of dark hair stopping at his pants, fiddling with the button but not popping it open.

His cock was a rigid line straining the fabric of his pants, and he groaned, shifting under me.

"Would you like me to set him free?" I asked, my voice low and sultry.

"God, yes," he rasped, lifting his hips as if getting his crotch closer to me would speed up the process.

The article also said not to be afraid to ask questions, but I wasn't ready for that. My hands trembled, the only thing giving away my apprehension.

In a matter of seconds, I was about to see, touch, and hold Ethan's cock. I mentally shook my head, slid the button from its hole, and pulled the zipper down its track. My fingers tucked into the top of his boxer briefs, and the tip of my finger grazed the satiny skin of his head.

"Oh fuck," he grunted.

Wow. Just a light touch made him squirm in delight.

My pointer finger circled the cap of his dick, testing, and he released a stream of air from his lungs. It was strained, like he was trying to keep control.

I swallowed, then dragged his pants and boxers down his legs and folded them beside him. My teeth chewed my upper lip until I finally looked at him in all his naked glory.

His cock jutted out between his muscled thighs, thick and rigid. Unlike Joe, Ethan was circumcised, and his cock was paler, with tiny purple veins straining along the shaft.

And he was significantly larger. So big that my mouth filled with saliva imagining it stretching my sex wide open.

"You're wrecking me," he groaned, his heated gaze on me. "I could come just watching you eye-fuck me."

I licked my hand, wrapped it around his tip, and tugged.

"Oh God!" He threw his head back, the muscles along his chest and shoulders tensing. My palm took hold of him again and I pumped his heated rod. His teeth ground together as he breathed out slow and deep. He was a man desperately trying to maintain control.

I opened my mouth, slowly lowered myself, and blew moist breath over his shaft. He smelled of baby powder and soap. In a quick motion, I licked my tongue up the large vein, then sat back on my knees raking my gaze up his body.

Pleasure licked down my spine and landed between my legs. There was something about him spread out on the floor, naked, with his hands secured above his head.

"Please," he said, and warmth splayed across my lower back. Ooh, I liked it when he begged. "Take me in your mouth."

I scooped his cock up with my right hand, opened my mouth wide, and took him to the base of my throat. His hips flinched upward, and he screamed. It was guttural, and wetness seeped out of me in response to his intense pleasure.

I slid him out, his cock wet from my mouth, and circled my tongue over his bulbous head before I released him.

Then I did it again, my left hand massaging his balls, which were so tight the two had made one firm sac. I'd read this was a good sign. It meant his orgasm was nearing.

"Goddammit, baby. You're so good." He squirmed beneath me, the cuffs scraping against the leg of the desk.

I popped my lips off him and sat back.

"Why did you stop?" he asked, desperation in his eyes.

I shrugged. "I like when it twitches."

He glanced down at his swollen cock, the tip glistening with pre-cum.

His face was pained, but he said, "We can stop if you want."

My heart fluttered. He was in the heat of passion, his cock about to overflow, but he made sure I knew I could walk away.

I bit my lip. I had no intention of stopping this. I wouldn't have gone this far just to leave Ethan in misery. He wasn't Joe.

I was keeping Ethan on the brink of orgasm—the article called it edging—to make his release more intense.

It was empowering to give Ethan this kind of pleasure, but I wasn't doing it for him. I was doing it for me. Joe had talked so much shit about my lack of sexual prowess I wanted to prove to myself that I could be good at this.

But damn, I had no idea it would be so hot! My pussy pulsed, desperate to be stroked.

Lust. That's what this was. Pure, unadulterated lust.

*Patience, grasshopper,* I told myself. My time to come would come.

I wet my palm and wrapped Ethan's cock up like a birthday present, the delicate skin fevered. His face was contorted with a mix of pleasure and pain as he watched.

I jerked upward on his shaft, and he cried out, "Enough, baby. My balls are gonna burst. Finish me. Please."

I popped my hand off and met his gaze. His eyes were almost black, his pupils pushing out the color of his iris until it was a faint ring.

"You're in so much trouble when it's your turn," he grumbled.

I laughed and tilted over his hips, poking my tongue out and tracing the line between his taut balls. He sucked air in through his teeth, the muscles in his thighs contracting.

I sucked his hard sacs into my mouth one at a time, my tongue circling the rutty skin.

"Fucking hell." He yanked at the cuffs, but they stayed firmly around the desk. "This is torture."

"It'll be worth it," I said, hoping it was true.

My tongue glided up and around his rim, my saliva wetting him, and he raised his hips, begging me to put him out of his misery.

I tucked my lips over my teeth, wrapped my palm over his shaft again, and filled my mouth with him, suctioning him like a vacuum. My hand and mouth worked together as one unit, rubbing and sucking him.

"Oh fuck! Oh yes. Goddammit! I'm coming! I'm coming so hard!"

Ethan threw his head back and screamed. He actually screamed as if he'd been injured.

His hips convulsed, and a warm, salty liquid sprayed into my mouth, his cries unrestrained, the cuffs scraping the desk leg as his arms shook.

When his convulsions became soft trembles and his hips relaxed, I slid him out of my mouth and collapsed on the rug next to him.

Close, but not touching.

He gazed at the ceiling, awe and wonder in his glassy eyes.

"Baby, that was"—he turned his head toward me—"unfuckingbelievable."

My cheeks blossomed with color at his proclamation. No one had ever said anything like that to me. And I'd swallowed. I never did that. I always ran to the bathroom and spit, washing out my mouth.

His gaze softened, and warm affection tapped inside my chest.

I turned my head away and sat up, buttoning my shirt.

"That was fun," I chirped and stood up. He was still attached to the desk, naked as a doornail.

I left him there.

"Evelyn," he called out, but I ignored him.

I changed and swiped toothpaste over my teeth, then gathered my items and finally came back into the office.

"Where are you going?" he asked, frowning.

I kept my eyes on his face. My sex was begging for him to finish what we'd started, and if his kiss told me anything, it was that I'd be screaming louder than he had when I came.

"Home," I said.

"But—"

"Here." I leaned over and clicked the button that released the cuffs. He stood, not bothering to put his clothes on.

His gaze darkened. "I don't leave women unsatisfied."

A laugh popped out of me, coupled with a tingle of excitement, which meant I had to leave. Now.

"I can satisfy myself."

Heat rushed up his neck and face, coloring his skin. My eyes flicked down. His spent cock was at half-mast on the way to fully erect.

"I think you may need to take care of yourself again."

He frowned. "Come on, Evelyn. Don't run away."

"I'm not." I bristled.

I absolutely was.

I bent down and threw his clothes at him, which he caught in one arm and held against his side.

"Next time it's my turn to make you scream," he yelled at my retreating back.

"We'll see," I said, a smile on my face.

The moment I was safely back at my apartment, I shoved my hands in my panties and had the best fucking orgasm of my life.

# Chapter 16

## *Eva*

I was at work staring at my computer, but all my attention was on my phone next to my keyboard. How could one small piece of technology hold so much power over me?

Five days ago it meant nothing.

Now it held the power of Ethan. And I hated it. I didn't want any man to have this kind of stronghold on my emotional state.

I'd left Ethan's apartment elated, feeling vindicated for everything Joe had put me through. I'd taken my power back and said fuck you to him and his lies.

Two could play this game.

Or three.

Then there was the cherry on top—it had been an unbelievable sexual experience. Most of the focus had been on Ethan (my choice), but I'd never been that stimulated, and I was eager to do it again. Bigger. Better. And oh yeah, wetter.

Except I hadn't heard a damn thing from Ethan.

It had been a week. Seven days. One hundred and sixty-eight hours. And nothing. Not even a stupid emoji text or a like on one of my social media posts.

We weren't together. We weren't dating. This was revenge fucking, but I figured having his cock in my mouth would warrant some type of communication post-suckle. I almost preferred when we were enemies. At least, I knew where I stood.

All the ickiness that I'd wallowed in as a child when my dad would sayonara Mom and me was gurgling in every cell, and I was nauseous.

I'd made it clear from the beginning that this was nothing more than sexual warfare, but I was a woman with emotions, and it was a bit worrying that he had been incommunicado.

*Enough! I shall think on it no longer.*

If Ethan was done with all this, fine. FINE! There were other ways to get revenge on Joe without Ethan.

My phone pinged, and I nearly knocked my tea over to grab it.

It was Joe.

*Hey, babe. I grabbed a bento box from Shuko. I'll be there in 5.*

I banged my phone on my desk. Joe mentioned coming by for lunch today, but I'd thought he was placating me for standing me up for dinner on Sunday night and would cancel.

Normally, I'd eat at my desk, but the company

encouraged us to take brain breaks and "fill our well" every few hours. Another reason I loved this place.

My forehead fell in my hands. *Ugh*.

I didn't want to start over and search for another job that was as supportive and compassionate. My colleagues cared about civic and social issues and worked hard but knew when to stop and play and have fun.

No matter what Joe tried to do, I would find a way to stay. I didn't want to game the system, and there was a little part of me that felt guilty, but it wasn't my damn fault Joe decided to end our marriage before it began.

On the main floor, there was a communal cafeteria. I told Joe to meet me there. It was better than parading him around the office. I hated playing the happy couple in front of my colleagues.

He was sitting at one of the wooden booths along the long row of floor-to-ceiling windows that looked out onto the busy streets when I walked in. My bento box was open and ready for me to eat with chopsticks and soy sauce, a La Croix poured over ice in a glass.

When I spotted him, my spidey senses went on high alert. He only did nice stuff like this when he wanted something. Even before his affair with Ashley, he rarely went out of his way for me unless it benefited him in some capacity.

Another red flag I'd ignored.

"Aren't you eating?" I asked.

He tugged at his still-too-tight pants. "I had a keto shake earlier."

I bit the inside of my cheek to keep from smirking.

"How's the build going?" I asked.

Joe exhaled loudly and slumped his shoulders. "Lots of last-minute problems."

I nodded. Joe had been complaining about this for the past few days.

"I can't continue like this," Joe grunted. "It's not good for my health. I think that's why I've gotten fat. My cortisol levels are off because of stress."

Which was BS because he wasn't fat. He was as trim and defined as always, but his pants had shrunk, unbeknownst to him.

"Your work has always been like this. Maybe you need more downtime," I said, shoveling a piece of sashimi into my mouth.

"That's not the issue. I live too far from the work sites. It's becoming too hard to commute."

My chopsticks hovered over my spicy salmon roll.

"It wasn't a problem before." I put my chopsticks down and took a sip of my drink, trying to keep my voice level. But I feared he was about to drop a grenade, and I was trying to figure out what to do.

"It is now," he hissed, his cheeks burning red.

A wave of fury slammed into me. I was so over his selfishness and the games he continued to play with me and my life.

"That's too fucking bad, Joe," I snapped. "Be a grown-up and figure it out."

My hands shook, and I clasped them together to stop the tremble.

His eyes widened in surprise, and it took him several long moments to find words.

"I am figuring it out," he whined, a tinge of annoyance in his tone. "I think we should move up—"

"We're not moving," I cut him off. "We sat down for hours and mapped out what we would and would not compromise when we moved to the city, and moving upstate was a hard no for me." I narrowed my gaze. "Would you like me to pull up the document? I have it in my saved documents."

My mom paid for us to go to a pre-marriage counselor who took us through the main issues that drove couples apart—kids, religion, money, infidelity, place of residency.

"I'm not a child. I don't need you to show me the fucking document," Joe spat. Then he sat back and leveled his gaze.

My skin prickled.

"With all this extra work and living so far away, I can't go to your interview."

My knees shot up and hit the table, rattling the tray in front of me.

"You have to be there." My voice wobbled. The interview couldn't happen without him. The immigration officer had to interview us together.

He shrugged. "I can't. I need to be at the site that day."

I felt the color drain from my face, and I was about to remind him that his boss had already agreed to give him the time off, but I stopped myself.

143

Instead, I said, "I'll see if I can change the date."

My chest rose and fell rapidly, and Joe held back a smile. "Thanks, babe." He put his hand over mine and squeezed.

I ground my teeth, the fury so hot I almost screamed in his face. He still wanted to discard me and ship me back up to Canada so he could be with Ashley, and I would be out of the way, but I had an idea.

When Joe left, I'd call his boss and make sure he knew exactly when the interview was. Then Joe couldn't show up to work that day or he'd alert his boss to his lie.

I cleared my throat and searched for a topic to distract me from my outrage.

"Have you heard from Ethan lately?" I asked. "I've been trying to get in touch with him."

Joe was flicking through his phone, barely listening.
"Joe?"

"Huh." He glanced up.

"Ethan. What's going on with him?"

"Why are you contacting him?" Joe asked, frowning.

"My boss had a question about his foundation," I quickly lied.

Joe scoffed, but then he bolted upright.

"Wait. What's the date?" Joe glanced at his watch. "Oh shit. It's Ethan's birthday tomorrow."

"So?" I said, packing up my sushi. I wasn't hungry anymore.

"His dad always visits during his birthday."

Joe shoved his phone in his back pocket and stood, his face set with determination.

"Where are you going?" I asked, hurrying after Joe.

"To Ethan's."

I ran out the door and down the subway steps, following Joe into a waiting train traveling downtown.

"Why?" I knew Ethan's childhood hadn't been great, but I didn't know exactly what had made it so horrible besides his parents not liking each other.

"His old man used to hit him. He got sober and supposedly changed, but he's still a piece of shit. His dad always comes and sponges off him on his birthday, especially now that he's rich, and Ethan is too nice to tell him to fuck off."

The train halted. "Come on," Joe said, and we flew up the steps into TriBeCa.

For a moment I stood on the sidewalk, stunned by Joe's sudden passion to help his friend.

From childhood, Joe had taken on the role of the protector when it came to Ethan, and it hit me like a shot that part of the reason Joe was jealous of Ethan's success was that it meant Joe wasn't needed any longer. At least, in Joe's mind.

Saving Ethan from his father was familiar to Joe. It put the order of things right. He'd be the hero coming to rescue the damsel in distress again like he did when they were kids.

My heart twisted as I thought of Ethan as a child,

his father hurting him, and my feet ran faster, because even if he didn't need it, I wanted to help him. Joe had lost the privilege of being Ethan's defender, and I was suddenly determined to take this last scrap from Joe.

# Chapter 17

## *Ethan*

"What's on the agenda for the rest of your day?" my father, Ed, asked from his perch at the kitchen bar where he sipped his black coffee and read *The Post*.

He'd been here all week, but I was over it after one day.

"I have a work dinner with the new hires." I ground my teeth, holding back the curses in my head.

While he sat idly in my kitchen, all I wanted was him gone. Our relationship was better when there were hundreds of miles between us.

"Your Uber is gonna be here in an hour. Have you packed?" I asked.

He shrugged, keeping his eyes on the paper. "It'll take me five minutes."

Blood pumped rapidly through my veins, and I took three deep breaths as my therapist had taught me to do years ago. Until I saw my dad's ass walking out the door, the rock of anxiety in my gut wouldn't crack.

"Dad, we've had a nice visit. Don't fuck it up now."

Ed's hands tightened, crumpling the edges of the paper.

"I'm starving." Ed folded the paper roughly and then ran his hands through his thick, black hair. He was sixty-two, and his age was showing. His hair had begun to recede in the front and gray around the temples. The lines around his eyes had deepened, and his skin was a bit weathered, but he looked distinguished.

I had my dad's coloring, but my personality was all my mother's—calm and stubborn.

My phone trilled, indicating someone was ringing the building doorbell.

On the video screen were Joe and Eva.

A flash of Eva's mouth on my cock skittered into my brain, and my temperature spiked instantly.

I hesitated and then tapped on the phone screen, letting them in. What the hell were they doing here together? Did Joe know? Did Eva tell him?

The elevator door opened, and my gaze locked on Eva, trying to read clues on her face, but she looked away, searching the hall behind me.

The sight of her conjured up everything I'd been trying to forget all week—mainly, her mouth devouring my cock and driving me to the edge of sweet madness before I had the most insane orgasm of my life. *Fuck*. It had been glorious.

She wore a short, rainbow-patterned romper, the buttons down the front undone halfway, and goddammit she looked hot.

I fisted my hands in front of my pants, covering my cock's response, and flung my gaze toward Joe, waiting for him to explain their unexpected presence. The sight of him was like dipping my cock in ice water, and my hard-on disappeared.

"Where is the fucker?" Joe hissed.

"Who are you—oh," I said, realizing he meant my dad. "How did you—"

"Your birthday's tomorrow," he said as an explanation. I softened slightly. This was the Joe that had been my best friend. My father visited every year, and Joe always showed up like it was his duty.

Joe's home used to be my sanctuary, but I had my own place of refuge now, and I knew how to handle my father.

"Want me to get rid of him?" Joe asked, cracking his knuckles like we were in a bad gangster movie.

I held back a laugh. I really should've told Joe ages ago that I didn't need his help when it came to my father. Joe's intentions were noble, but he always caused more problems than solved.

Yeah, Ed had been a shit father—drank too much, sometimes raised a fist in my direction, verbally abusive —but I'd learned quickly how to stand up to him. He was mean to my mom but not abusive. That had been reserved for me.

It sucked, but by the time I got to high school, Ed

had sobered up, and without the alcohol and pills, the physical violence disappeared.

The only people that knew my father hit me were Joe's family, my therapist, and my ex, Jasmin. It was no one's damn business.

"Are you okay?" Eva looked up at me through her dark eyelashes, wariness in her eyes.

I ground my teeth, realizing Joe had told her about my father. I had no doubt that he'd played up his hero antics in whatever story he'd given her.

"He'll be fine now that we're here," Joe said. He slid his arm around Eva's waist and squeezed her to his side reassuringly.

"I don't need your help, man," I said, my voice harsher than I'd intended. "I can handle my father."

Joe's lips narrowed into a thin line, and he laughed sardonically. "All he wants is your money, and you cave every time. I'm just helping you have a backbone."

Fury spiked under my skin, and my right hand shot out and fisted Joe's collar. His arm was still around Eva, and she lost her footing and fell sideways, banging her knee against the entryway bench.

I released Joe and stepped back. What the fuck was wrong with me? I'd never fought with Joe. Not physically. But his snide remark and his arm around Eva made me see red.

Joe shoved me hard in the chest. My heels rocked back but I didn't push him in return.

"What the fuck, man?" He smoothed out his shirt where I'd grabbed it.

Eva was bent over, rubbing her knee. I reached out to her, but I quickly snatched my hand back.

"Are you okay?" I asked instead. "I didn't mean—"

"I'm fine," she snapped.

Every cell in me wanted to gather her up and assure her this had nothing to do with her.

"What's gotten into you?" Joe asked, wrapping his hand around Eva's shoulders protectively.

I shoved my hands through my hair, trying to get a grip on this situation and turn it around, but my head was clouded watching Joe comfort Eva as if he weren't the cause of her misery.

Fury had charged through my veins when I'd found her distraught in the bridal suite, and that anger had escalated with each new shitty thing Joe had done to her. Now he was playing the hero to my victim when he was the villain.

My body shook. I couldn't deal with Joe right now. And why was being this close to Eva so unbearable?

"Where are those fancy, fizzy sodas?" Ed called from the kitchen.

"In the mini fridge," I yelled back, mentally willing my dad not to come down the hallway.

Joe stepped forward, and I blocked his path to the kitchen.

"Thanks for checking in, but I'm good," I said and pressed the elevator button. The doors slid open.

"I'm gonna pack," Ed yelled from the back of the apartment. At least he'd be occupied until I could get Joe and Eva out of there.

"You should go. It's better if he doesn't see you. You two don't exactly bring out the best in each other."

"Something's going on with you, man. Ever since the wedding you've been weird."

*No shit.*

"I'm sorry you feel that way," I said.

*"I'm sorry you feel that way,"* Joe mocked. "You sound like a corporate douche. I liked you better before."

Joe didn't have to say it, but he was referring to my money. It was a strange beast that brought out the worst in some people.

Joe stepped into the elevator, but Eva stayed in the foyer, unmoving.

"Come on, babe," Joe said, crossing his arms.

"I'm gonna stay and chat with Ethan." Eva's voice was calm but—was it my imagination, or was there a burning heat behind her gaze?

"Remember? About that work thing," she said over her shoulder, not taking her eyes off me.

Joe's voice hardened. "Are you fucking kidding me right now?"

"I'll see you at home."

The moment the elevator shut, Eva pressed her hands on my shoulders and shoved me backward into the small bathroom. She kicked the door shut with her heel and slammed me against the closed door.

I opened my mouth to ask her what the hell was going on, but her lips covered mine, her tongue sliding inside before I could utter a word. Eva's tongue lapped mine, her mouth pillaging me like it was looking for lost treasure, and fire burned up my spine.

*Fuck, she felt good.*

My palms cupped her cheeks, meeting her kiss with a ravenous fervor. I'd dreamed of those lips all week, and now they were mine.

Her hips bumped against my groin, and I moaned. My cock had filled to capacity as soon as her body touched mine.

She popped her mouth off mine and licked down my neck, her tongue wet and warm.

"Fuck, Evelyn," I muttered as she continued her exploration, sucking on my collarbone and then gliding back up to my mouth.

We were all tongues and bodies rubbing together, revving up the fire she'd ignited with this kiss. My hands fisted her hair, tugging her closer.

Eva clasped my left hand and guided it under the shorts of her loose romper. I didn't need her to say what she wanted; I could feel the heat from between her thighs. My fingers snatched the crotch of her panties and roughly pulled them aside. My thumb grazed over her feminine lips, and a groan lodged in my throat when I felt her pussy dripping with wetness.

I flicked her clit, and she trembled against my chest as I slid two fingers inside her and pushed them to the hilt, finding that sensitive spot inside her while my thumb rubbed over her swollen nub.

Eva rocked her hips rhythmically against my hand as I finger-fucked her, her moans vibrating against my ribs.

"Oh God, Ethan. Right there." Her breathing had shallowed, her heart racing like a freight train between us.

My enflamed cock pressed painfully against the inside of my jeans, but I didn't care. This was about her. I'd take care of my need later. *After* I made her scream in ecstasy like she'd fucking done for me.

"I'm so close. Faster, Ethan," she panted, her voice almost a plea.

I was too lost in this moment—wrapped up in lust and desire—to question any of what was happening.

Eva gasped sharply, and her walls tightened around my fingers. I pressed my thumb harder into her clit, rubbing fiercely in circles, desperate for her to catch fire in my hands.

Eva tipped her head back and screamed out. I pressed my mouth over hers, muffling her cries as she trembled in my arms. I pumped my fingers in unison with her convulsions, and I almost came right there in my pants, overcome by the sounds of her erupting.

Her head collapsed against my neck, her breath hot on my skin. My fingers slid out, wet with her moisture.

"That was amazing," she said, a small smile on her lips. Her gaze dropped to the aching bulge between my thighs.

"You look like I felt last week when I left here," she said wryly. "I barely made it in my front door before I touched myself and screamed out my orgasm."

"Fucking hell, Evelyn," I cursed. My balls tightened to the point of pain, and I buckled over.

I couldn't tell if what we'd just done was part of the game or something new, but at the moment, I couldn't give a fuck because I needed her to leave so I could jerk off.

"Go, Evelyn. Now." The words were strangled, my fingers itching to give my cock relief.

"I wanna watch you." Her voice was soft, almost a whisper.

I didn't hesitate. I popped open the buttons of my jeans and yanked them down to my knees, and I sighed loudly as my cock sprung out.

I licked my palm, wrapped it around my rock-hard erection, and groaned in sweet relief.

I squeezed my cock hard, pumping almost violently. In three strokes, my orgasm buzzed through my balls, up my shaft, and rocketed out of my cock.

"Oh God. Oh fucking hell!"

I fell forward, my left hand gripping the sink as liquid shot out, hitting the floor and cabinet, my orgasm ripping me apart.

I convulsed and cursed and nearly blacked out as the semen pumped out of me until I was panting over the cold marble, boneless.

"That was so hot," Eva whispered, her lips tickling my ear. "I'll be thinking of you fisting your cock when I'm in bed tonight."

I grunted at the thought of her hands on her pussy.

She leaned forward and kissed me gently on the cheek.

"Happy birthday." Then she slid out of the bathroom, the door clicking behind her.

# Chapter 18

## *Eva*

The immigration services office was in Lower Manhattan in a monolith skyscraper with long rectangular windows cascading up and down the front. For something that held so much power, it was surprisingly unremarkable.

The interview was in an hour, and if it all went smoothly, my citizenship would soon be official. I sipped the last of my decaf coffee and tossed it in the trash as I entered the building.

In the lobby, I paced the gray speckled tiles, unable to sit, until Joe arrived.

After Joe said he couldn't make the interview, I emailed his boss and gently reminded him of the exact day and time of the interview.

As expected, his boss had been very accommodating and wished us luck.

Joe had been furious when he found out I'd contacted his boss, but when I reminded him that getting my citizenship was a good thing for us, he stalked off and didn't say anything else about it.

I checked my phone again. There were messages from Rachel and my mom wishing me luck. There was even one from Ethan, but none from Joe.

It was surprising that Ethan cared at all. Obviously, he cared on some level. A man can't do what Ethan did to me and feel nothing.

My mind wandered to the toe-curling orgasm Ethan had given me. It was two weeks ago when I'd screamed in ecstasy in his guest bathroom, but my body responded to the memory, my pussy clenching.

I'd practically skipped home from Ethan's apartment, elated. Who knew a revenge affair could be so empowering?

When Joe and I stepped into Ethan's entryway that day, it was like an electric current had yanked me toward him. While Joe was self-righteously trying to protect Ethan from his father—which had been bullshit —every cell in my body wanted to wrap around Ethan, to touch him, and to be touched by him.

The moment we'd been alone it was like a madwoman had taken over. I could barely contain my animalistic lust.

*Fuuuuck*...I nearly fainted when Ethan gathered me up with the same ravenous need that had been coursing through me while I stood in that hallway.

It took everything in me not to text him afterward and beg him to finish what we'd started. My sex tingled, yearning to know what it felt like to be filled by him, but we aren't playing this game to fill a sexual need. It was to wreck Joe when the time came. But why not have a little fun while we waited for that moment?

I glanced at the time on my phone, and everything dropped out of my mind. *Where the hell was he?*

The interview was in ten minutes. I called Joe again, but it went straight to voice mail. He was traveling from upstate on the train, and he should've been out of the subway by now.

He'd planned to come home last night so we could travel to the appointment together, but by dinner, he'd texted and said he'd meet me here instead. He had some excuse about the architect giving him trouble and him needing to stay upstate.

My stomach churned, and I breathed through the urge to vomit. I walked into the elevator and texted Joe to come straight up to the appointment.

I walked to the man behind the window partition, gave him my name, and explained that my husband was late. The man told me to let him know when we were both there.

I waited over an hour, but Joe never came.

* * *

I slumped on a bench in a small park two blocks from the immigration building, the midday sun high above the trees.

Little spikes of fury pricked under my skin and I

gripped my phone until my knuckles turned white. My dozens of texts and phone calls to him were unanswered.

The fucker had screwed me over. Again.

I'd made up an excuse and rescheduled the appointment, but it meant I had to wait even longer to rid myself of this toxic relationship and finally set course on a new path.

I rubbed my throat, the pressure of my unknown future physically strangling me.

I slammed my phone down on the bench and squeezed my eyes shut, trying to make sense of all this.

Something brushed my thigh, and I looked up just in time to see a teenage boy snatch my phone and run across the park. I shot up and ran after him, screaming that he'd taken my phone. Pedestrians glanced at me but did nothing. Not shocking in this city.

The kid jumped over the short fence that lined the park and crossed the street, dodging cars. I clambered over the fence, but my purse strap caught the top of it and yanked me backward. I stumbled and landed hard on my knees.

Pain shot through my legs. I limped forward and crossed the street, blood dripping down both shins, but the kid was gone.

I reached into my purse to call the police, but then I remembered that punk had stolen my phone.

A cab with its light on was moving toward me and I put my hand out, debating where to go. I didn't know where Rachel was, and I had no way of getting in touch with her or anyone.

I gave the cabbie the address of my office. It was closest, and I could clean up and use the office phone to call Rachel. My brain was in too much of a fog to think clearly beyond the next step. She'd know what to do.

My heart wrapped around that thought warmly. I wanted my best friend.

At the building, I took the elevator to my floor and scurried to my normal spot at the worktable, hoping to avoid anyone asking questions if they saw my knees. I stopped short. There were little American flags and red, white, and blue balloons decorating the space. Two of my work colleagues, Peyton and Jackson, noticed me and walked over.

"How did it go?" Peyton asked, a wide smile on her face. "We didn't expect you until late—"

She stopped speaking, and her eyes widened into saucers when she saw my knees.

"Oh my God. Eva!" Peyton said, alarmed. "What happened?"

"Derrick!" Jackson yelled across the office, then turned back to me. "Are you okay?"

"I'm fine," I said, but my throat constricted, tightening around the lie.

"Did this happen at the office?" Jackson asked. A valid question since he was the company lawyer.

"No."

Derrick's heavy footfalls signaled his approach,

and his analytical gaze scanned my disheveled appearance.

"Get the first aid kit," Derrick commanded in that authoritative way he had about him. Peyton slid her hand into Jackson's and squeezed, then he left to retrieve it.

They were the company lovebirds, but I rarely saw them show public affection in the office. Although Peyton would sometimes come out of Jackson's closed office a little disheveled and rosy-cheeked, a small smile on her lips.

"Tell me what happened," Derrick said, drawing my attention.

Without faltering, I told him about the kid that had taken my phone and how I'd fallen down chasing after him.

"Never chase. It's not worth it," Derrick said, tapping his phone screen. "You could've been stabbed or worse."

"Okay." I sniffed.

Derrick lifted the phone to his ear as it rang.

"This is really nice." I lifted my shoulder toward all the patriotic decorations, but Derrick didn't hear me. He was on the phone speaking rapidly to someone.

"It was Derrick's idea," Peyton said, holding out a bottle of water. I drank from it greedily.

"Do you have Find My Phone?" he asked me, pulling the phone away from his mouth.

"Yes."

"Give me your number and password and the police can track it if it's still on."

I did as instructed. The next thirty minutes were a whirlwind of activity. While Derrick and his old police colleagues were investigating this minor crime, I used Peyton's phone to text Rachel, and within ten minutes she was there.

Rachel stepped out of the elevator and hugged me, and I bit my bottom lip to keep from crying.

"What happened to your knees?" she asked. They were cleaned and bandaged now.

"I fell on them while I chased the kid. Stupid, I know."

"The kid's an amateur." Derrick rolled his chair over to us. "He kept the phone on, and it was tracked to a bodega on the Lower East Side where a group of teenagers were hanging out, including the one that took your phone."

Rachel shook her head as she knelt before me, inspecting my knees. "The police did all that for a phone?"

"It was a slow day," Derrick said. "Plus this is how major criminals are caught a lot of the time. They commit some petty crime and get busted. Not in this case. It was a kid. But this isn't his first offense."

"Oh," I said, cringing as Rachel accidentally bumped my knee. She mouthed *sorry*. "Do they have my phone?"

"Yes. You'll need to go down to the station and give a statement." Derrick handed me a piece of paper with the address. "It won't take long. Get your phone and go home and rest and take tomorrow off."

* * *

Back at my place, Rachel leaned into the open fridge.

"There's no food," Rachel said, snatching a bottle of white wine and pulling two glasses from the cabinet.

She unscrewed the top, filled the glasses to the brim, and handed me one. I took a large sip, still wound up after our trip to the police station.

My phone was plugged in next to me. It had run out of battery at some point between the police finding it and me traveling downtown to give my statement.

"There's soup in the pantry," I said. "And crackers."

My phone powered on and pinged with several messages. There were texts from friends and family asking about the interview, but not one message was from Joe. Disappointment fell on me like a cold blanket. Nothing. It was nearly five. How was he going to talk his way out of this one?

My phone rang in my hand, and I startled. It was Ethan.

"'ello," I said over a yawn.

"I've been trying Joe and you all day. Was everything okay with the interview?"

I rested my head on the back of the sofa cushion and closed my eyes.

"It didn't happen. Joe never came, and I can't get in touch with him," I said.

"Fuck," Ethan growled. He was quiet for a long moment, but I could hear his ragged breathing. "What happens now? Will you have to move back?"

"I made up a lie about Joe's train being delayed and I was able to reschedule the interview," I said.

"Thank God," Ethan said, relief in his voice.

"Yeah. It's been a shit day, but it's better now." I leaned forward and sipped my wine. "Rachel's taking care of me."

"Did something else happen?"

I told him about my phone being stolen and falling and going to the station to report it.

"I feel sorry for the kid. He's barely thirteen, and the cop said it was his third offense and he could go to juvenile detention." I breathed out roughly through my nose, remembering the young teenager sitting next to his grandmother in the lobby of the station. The cop who interviewed me pointed him out. "I doubt that's gonna help him. And his grandmother looked like a ton of bricks were on her shoulders."

"You didn't do anything wrong," Ethan said, his voice hard. "That was his choice."

"I know. I'm just tired and hungry." I don't know why, but I added, "And lonely. Like in my bones."

Rachel squeezed my hand, and my chin wobbled.

"Fuck. I better go." I laughed over the wetness in my throat. "I'm feeling sorry for myself. I'll talk to you later."

I hung up and curled up in a ball on the couch as Rachel opened a can of tomato soup. She split it between two bowls with a handful of Ritz crackers.

I'd taken two bites of the sad dinner when the intercom buzzed. Rachel pressed the speaker button, and it crackled to life.

"Delivery from Nobu," came a young woman's voice.

Rachel glanced at me, and I shrugged my shoulders.

"We didn't order any food," Rachel said.

"It's for Evelyn Hart," the woman said. "From Mr. Ethan Steele. He asked me to deliver it personally. I'm Shaalani, one of the managers at the Midtown location."

Rachel mouthed *oh my God* to me and buzzed her up. Shaalani was dressed in a little black dress and platform shoes, and her arms were weighed down by several brown bags.

"Hi." Shaalani smiled widely and set out a large selection of dishes and gave detailed descriptions of each one. She placed a small card with her number on the counter. "If you have any issues, please call me immediately."

As soon as she left, I picked up my phone and shot a text to Ethan.

*You didn't have to do this. But thank you. xo*

I immediately received a text back.

*You needed something and I could provide it. It's what friends do. xx*

I stared at my phone as warmth settled in my chest.

"Everything okay?" Rachel asked, shoveling noodles into her mouth.

"Yeah," I mumbled, the smell of the food stirring me out of my trance. "It's perfect."

# Chapter 19

## *Ethan*

I paced my terrace, gripping the little bundle—my new nephew—to my shoulder. He slept peacefully against my neck, his warm breath a calming salve on my nerves.

It took everything in me not to storm out of the apartment, find Joe, and strangle his pathetic neck. That motherfucker.

My Apple watch pinged with a text from Shaalani, informing me that the food from Nobu had been delivered.

"What the hell is going on?" My sister, Savi, sat on the gray sectional, her feet kicked up on the driftwood coffee table. Inside, her older child, my niece, Brynn, slept in the guest room. The terrace door was open so we could hear her if she woke up, but it was after six and she should be down for the night.

I sank into the oversized cushion next to Savi, careful not to disturb little Beau, and exhaled roughly.

"Please tell me you're not in love with your best friend's wife," my sister said.

"Hell no," I balked. "I'm furious at Joe. He slept with Jasmin and now he's cheating on Evelyn and trying to wreck her life."

Savi squeezed my hand and frowned. "You don't have to fix everyone, you know. Let that childhood pattern go."

I snorted a humorless laugh. My sister was a therapist and liked to get to the core of a person's behavior.

"Fuck. I'm so predictable." I sighed, but the strangle of worry didn't release. Joe may have just wrecked Eva's citizenship.

Beau gurgled and shifted in my arms, stretching his little legs inside his swaddle. I kissed his fuzzy head and gently placed him in the bassinet on the cushion next to me. My heart swelled in my chest. Man, I loved this little guy.

My niece and nephew were blessings I never knew I needed. After the mess that was my childhood, it was awesome to be part of a family where the children hadn't just been wanted but planned for meticulously.

My sister was fifteen years older than me, nearly forty. My parents had barely been keeping their marriage together, waiting to divorce once my sister graduated high school, but then I came along. An unwelcome accident.

My sister said it was a miracle I was even born. My parents barely spoke to each other and slept in different rooms. If I wasn't a mirror image of my dad, I'd question my paternity.

They stayed together after I was born, believing that parents who were married and miserable were better than parents who were separated and happy.

It was no wonder my sister never married, but she'd always wanted kids, and through the miracle of modern fertility, she had her babies using her best friend's husband's sperm.

"There's nothing wrong with wanting to help people," Savi said. "But you know the saying... *You make plans and God laughs.*"

I shrugged. Yeah, I liked things orderly. Except... ever since I'd gotten into this thing with Eva, my life had been spectacularly out of control. But somehow, I didn't mind. Not when I was with her. Her unpredictability had become an unexpected turn-on.

I looked out across the low skyline of SoHo as the sun dipped behind the buildings. My sister crossed her arms, waiting for me to speak more about what had been going on with Eva.

"I'm not trying to fix Evelyn, I'm—"

"Why do you always call her Evelyn?" my sister interrupted.

Pressure filled my chest.

"Out of respect," I said, averting my eyes. "She said she wanted to go by Evelyn when I first met her. She thought it sounded more professional when applying for jobs. Joe laughed it off and didn't even try. Eventually, everyone went back to Eva but... I don't know." I shrugged. "I liked how she smiled when I'd call her that."

"So you've always liked her," Savi said matter-of-factly.

"No." I bristled.

"Did she annoy you or did it annoy you that she was with Joe and not you?"

"No," I said quickly.

"Yeah, right." Savi nudged my shoulder. "Come on."

"I'm serious. I didn't like her. I thought she was using Joe, and it pissed me off."

"Tell me more about that. Why did it upset you? You never cared about Joe's other girlfriends." Savi tilted her head, her neon-red hair brushing my arm. Her natural color was dirty-blonde, but she'd dyed it just after Beau was born. It was so vivid it nearly glowed.

Beau whimpered next to me, his arm coming free from his swaddle. I tucked it back in and turned back to Savi, trying to figure out what the hell to tell her. I wasn't even sure what the answers were anymore.

"Can you be my sister right now and not a therapist?" I asked.

"Fine. How did you suddenly become so cozy with *Evelyn*?"

"How do you mean?"

"You just sent food to her from a five-star restaurant because she had a bad day." Savi raised her eyebrows. "Spill."

"We have a common goal, and we're working together to reach it," I said.

"What goal?"

There was no point avoiding it, so I started at the beginning.

"I found out about Jasmin and Joe right before the wedding. The only reason I didn't punch his lights out was because of the upcoming nuptials." I rubbed my temples. "All that fury had been simmering, so when Evelyn suggested a revenge pact, I jumped at it."

I threw my hands up in the air, unable to put all the uneasiness that gnawed at my gut into words.

"It was fun at first, but now I'm all confused about it."

Savi chewed her bottom lip, studying me with her discerning gaze. "Because you started having feelings for her."

"That's not what I said." My cock loved being with Eva, I knew that much, but I wasn't ready to dive deeper into my emotional reservoir for answers. "Anyway, Joe is about to fuck up Evelyn's life, and I'm not gonna let him."

Savi rolled her eyes. "Eva doesn't need you to save her. She can handle her own life. If she doesn't get her citizenship, she'll be okay. Yeah, it would suck for a bit, and she'd have to move out of the country and find a new job in Canada, but from what I know of Eva, she's a fighter."

Anxiety squeezed my organs. Savi was right. Eva would thrive no matter what she did.

"I know Eva will be fine. But..." Fury rose up my throat, constricting my words. "She shouldn't have to start over because Joe's an asshole," I ground out. "He needs a good kick in the nuts, and I want to give it to him."

Savi put her hands up in resignation. "Fine. But I'll be here to say I told you so when it all goes belly-up."

I smiled tightly because she was right. This could only end badly. I was pretty sure Eva knew this too. But I couldn't stop this train.

Eva—and Joe's deceptions—consumed my thoughts.

My fingers itched to text her. I wanted to talk to her and comfort her and know what she was thinking. Had Joe called and given her some shitbag excuse? Did Eva forgive him again or had she reached her limit?

I wasn't ready for our revenge games to be over.

My dick twitched thinking about her body against mine, little moans cascading from her mouth.

I shook my head. I had to stop that. Stop thinking about her that way.

Every day when my phone buzzed, I worried it would be a text from Eva or Joe, telling me it was over.

I wasn't ready for that. I wasn't ready for a life that didn't have Eva in it.

# Chapter 20

## *Eva*

The phone call came in the middle of the night. It knocked me out of my restless sleep, and I slapped my hand on the nightstand until I gripped my phone. I didn't recognize the number but answered it anyway because no one called me in the middle of the night.

"'Ello?" I asked, my voice sticky. Rachel and I had drunk several glasses of wine while we enjoyed the delicacies from Nobu earlier that night.

The woman on the phone was wailing, and I bolted upright, alert.

"Who...who is this?" I asked, unable to recognize the voice through her crying.

The woman spoke again, but her voice was garbled, her words swallowed by her distress.

"Slow down. I can't understand you," I said, my chest tightening. The woman sounded too young to be Joe's mother. And it wasn't Rachel or my mom. There was no one else who would call me in the middle of the night.

She took a deep breath, her voice steady.

"Joe was in an accident," she said, every word crystal clear.

Goose bumps erupted over my skin, and I shook my head as if I could shake a sentence out.

"What?" I asked.

"He fell off a roof and hit his head. They can't wake him. He—" The woman's voice cracked, and she dissolved into tears again.

"Who is this?" I asked, my ears ringing.

"Ashley."

I tensed, anger flaring up over my confusion, but the need for answers overwhelmed my shock.

"Where are you?" I swung my feet to the rug and gathered my clothes from yesterday which were strewn around the floor. I pulled and yanked them on as I listened.

"The staff won't tell me anything because I'm not family." More tears and gulps of air.

"Where is he?" I asked.

"They took him to, uh, Phillips Hospital."

Thoughts rushed through my head unbidden. *How long has Joe been there? Why is Ashley with him? Where are my shoes? Do I need to call his parents? Is he dead? How do I get upstate at midnight?*

"I'm on my way." I spun around, trying to sort through the cluster of thoughts that spun a web in my mind.

I'd spent all night talking smack about Joe to Rachel, but what if he hadn't sabotaged me on purpose? Oh God. I'd been cursing him out while he was injured in the hospital.

I was a monster. I was a horrible, horrible gremlin.

I opened my contacts and called Rachel. "Help."

"Where are you?" Her voice was startled but calm. In the background I heard loud, garbled voices and the bass of electronic dance music.

"Joe's in the hospital. In Westchester. I...I..."

"Where are you?" she asked again.

"At my apartment."

"Get your bag, phone, and charger and meet me out front. I'm coming."

Twenty minutes later, a black town car pulled up and Rachel rolled down the window of the back door.

"Get in." She opened the door, and I slid in next to her. She handed me a banana. "Eat this."

I did as I was told robotically. The car lurched forward, and streetlights streaked past the windows as we drove across the avenue. Then we entered the freeway, and blackness surrounded me.

Something warm enveloped my hand. I looked down. It was Rachel's hand on mine. It shook me out of my stupor, and I blinked at her.

"How did you get this car?" I asked. There was a little stencil on the plastic partition between us and the driver that read *Ray's Limo Service. Private Luxury Cars for Corporate Hire.*

"It doesn't matter," she said. Her hair was in

braided pigtails, she had red glitter on her eyelids, and she wore a tiny black leather skirt, red fishnets, knee pads, and a torn roller derby team shirt.

"You were at a match?" I asked. "After all that drinking?"

"I called the hospital," Rachel said, ignoring my question. "I found out more information."

"How? They wouldn't tell Ashley anything." Bile inched up my esophagus at the thought of Ashley being by Joe's side while I was alone in bed, furious at him.

"I called and pretended I was you," Rachel said. We made a sharp left off the freeway and turned onto a highway that runs along the Hudson River.

"What did they say?" I asked.

"Joe's stable but in serious condition," Rachel said.

"What does that mean?" I asked, swallowing over the lump lodged in my throat. I was furious at Joe, but I didn't want him gravely injured.

"Is he going to—" A strangled cry escaped my throat, and tears rolled down my cheeks. "Die?"

Rachel held my arm. "No."

"Did they say what happened?" I dropped my head in my hands and rubbed my temples, trying to focus. "Why is Ashley there?"

"I don't know why she's there, babe." Rachel pulled me into her side and held me. "The nurse said he slipped off a roof and hit his head on the edge of a truck bed. He was unconscious when he arrived at the hospital. That's all they'd tell me over the phone."

I bolted upright. "I have to call his parents."

The car swung to the left, and we pulled into the hospital parking lot, the driver following signs toward the emergency room entrance.

"Wait until you speak to the doctor and have more information. Then call them," Rachel said as we pulled under the portico.

The woman at the reception desk sent us to the trauma ICU where Joe was being treated. When we entered his room and pulled back the curtain, we saw Ashley sitting on a chair, bent over his bed.

Multiple tubes and needles were attached to Joe's body, and his head was wrapped in white gauze.

When Ashley heard us enter, she turned. Her face was void of makeup, her eyes puffy and her cheeks red.

"Oh, thank God." She wrapped her arms around me, and I tensed. "They won't tell me anything. I had to beg them to let me stay in here until you arrived."

I let her cry on me, but when her sobs turned into soft whimpers, I lifted her off and moved her to the chair.

The door opened and a middle-aged woman with skin as dark as midnight walked in wearing scrubs. She held a clipboard and slid her wire-rimmed glasses up her nose.

"Are you Mrs. Patell?" she asked me.

I nodded.

"I'm Dr. Spencer," she said, glancing at her notes.

"Is he going to be okay?" Ashley asked before I could say anything.

Dr. Spencer glanced between Ashley and me.

"May I speak freely?" she asked, directing her question to me.

"Yes," I said, my voice wobbling. Rachel stepped closer to my side.

"Your husband has a traumatic brain injury which caused intracranial hematoma or bleeding in the brain. We've given him medicine through his IV to stop the bleeding. We'll need to monitor him over the next few days."

Tears leaked out of my eyes as she spoke, and Ashley sniffled where she sat in the chair.

"When will he wake up?" I asked.

"His condition is serious, which means we need to monitor him and wait for the medicine to work and for the swelling to go down. Then we'll know more."

A nurse knocked on the door, spoke quietly to the doctor, then left.

"Look." Dr. Spencer held the door open with her foot, ready to exit. "I'd love to give you definitive answers, but brain injuries are unpredictable. I know it's hard, but waiting is the only way to know more. His vitals are stable, and he's young and healthy. That gives me hope."

The door clicked shut, and I walked to Joe's side. A tube was stuck in his nose, and there was a nasty bruise forming over his temple, blood pooling under his skin at the side of his left eye. His face was slack and child-like. My hand gripped his shoulder, and I pressed a kiss to his cheek.

"I'm here, Joe. It's Eva. I'm right here," I whispered into his ear, hoping the sound of my voice would give him some comfort.

I held on to him, but a thought crashed into me— *What if it's not me he wants comfort from? What if it's Ashley?*—and my knees buckled. I sank to the floor and buried my face in the side of the bed, the thought eviscerating me.

I whipped around to face her. "What are you doing here?"

Ashley's bloodshot eyes widened. "His work called me. I guess I'm still his emergency contact."

I narrowed my gaze. "Why didn't you tell them to call me? Why did you come here?" I asked. "You and Joe haven't been together for years. I'm his wife."

Her mouth opened and shut, and she glanced at Rachel for help. Rachel crossed her arms and raised an eyebrow, offering nothing.

"I..." Ashley crumpled, her chin dropping to her chest. "I'm so sorry, Eva. We didn't mean to...I... I'm so sorry."

I stilled, my blood turning to ice. Was she apologizing for the affair? She didn't come out and say it, but her words were wrapped in the guilt of it.

My hands cupped my ears, not wanting to hear her confession, unable to deal with her guilt on top of my grief.

"Get out," I hissed.

"What? But I want to—"

"Out!" I screeched, my skin burning. "Get her the fuck out of here!"

Ashley's face filled with horror, and the nurse—who'd come in when I began to scream—gently pulled her out of the room.

I dissolved into tears and pulled my knees to my chest until I was a tight ball. I was vaguely aware of Rachel coming into the room and pulling a chair up next to me, laying my head on her shoulder, and petting my hair until my breathing slowed.

"I don't know what to feel. I don't know what to do. What do I do, Rach?" I hiccupped, never-ending tears cascading down my cheeks. "This can't be happening. He has to be all right."

"Just rest." Rachel kissed my temple. "All we can do is wait."

# Chapter 21

## *Ethan*

I sat tensely at the edge of my sofa, gripping my hands together in front of me in one fist. Rachel had called an hour ago with the news that Joe was hurt and in the hospital and asked me to send a car to pick her and Eva up to drive them upstate to the hospital. Without hesitation, I ordered a car from my service. I had no idea how Rachel got my number, but it didn't matter.

My first instinct was to go with them to the hospital, but something stopped me.

I was all jumbled, my mind short-circuiting. It felt like fists were squeezing my organs.

Joe had been a bastard to Eva and me, that was true, but it didn't lessen the fear that gripped me when I thought of him being injured in the hospital.

"What are you doing up?" My sister walked into the room, bleary-eyed, and sank into the sofa, Beau in her arms. She unhooked the strap of her sleeper tank top, and I glanced away as she shifted Beau onto her breast.

"Joe's in the hospital." I stood, pacing around my living room. "I sent a car for Eva to take her there, but I don't know what to do. *Motherfucker*."

I slammed my fist against the wall, the flat-screen TV rattling on its mount. Beau startled and whimpered. Savi jiggled him, and he nestled back into her chest, suckling.

"Sorry," I said.

"Why aren't you at the hospital?" Savi asked through a yawn.

"I want to go. I mean, what if it's the worst and I'm not there because of some petty grudge?"

Savi blinked and widened her eyes a couple of times as if to wake herself up. "It's not petty. He fucked the love of your life."

"Eva's not—" I automatically said.

"Jasmin," she interrupted, shaking her head. "But he is cheating on Eva. He hasn't been a saint. Just because he's in the hospital doesn't revolve him of his sins."

"Absolve," I corrected.

"Shurt urp." Savi stretched her right arm over her head. "I'm not even awake right now."

I rubbed my forehead roughly, my gut telling me to run to the hospital, but guilt and shame snaked inside my brain, confusing everything.

These were not emotions I was used to wrestling. My life was usually black and white. Right and wrong.

"Joe hurt you, but you can still care about him. Joe can fuck your ex, and you can still want to be with him when he's injured. Those feelings aren't mutually exclusive. We're not robots." Savi yanked a burp rag from the small pile of laundry next to her and threw it at me. "Now get the fuck out of here and go see your best friend. It doesn't mean you forgive him, but you'll never forgive yourself if the worst does happen and you didn't visit him."

I snatched my wallet from the coffee table and shoved it into my jeans pocket along with my phone, but I halted before I walked down the hallway.

"What if Eva's pissed I'm there?" I asked.

Savi rolled her eyes. "Go."

* * *

I ignored the nurse who called after me as I hurried past the entrance of the ER and tucked myself into the stairwell. I'd texted Rachel on my way upstate, and she gave me the room number and directions to the floor so I could sneak in. It was late. Long after midnight, way past visiting hours.

On the floor where the trauma ICU was located, I hurried down the hallway, past the empty nurses' station, and toward the patient rooms. When I found Joe's room, I stepped inside.

I stopped short.

Eva was curled in a ball in a chair, resting against Joe's bed. Her eyes were closed, but her cheeks were stained with fresh tears. Rachel sat in the corner on the small, beige sofa.

Rachel smiled softly, a knowing glint in her eyes that I ignored, and tipped her chin toward Eva, encouraging me to go to her, but my attention fell on Joe.

He was a solid guy, the result of him spending hours in the gym, but in the bed with blankets tucked under his armpits, an IV in his hand, oxygen in his nose, and his head bandaged, he looked small and vulnerable.

I ground my teeth, holding back a wave of panic that fisted in my throat.

"How is he?" I asked softly.

At my voice, Eva's eyes flew open, and she flung herself at me. I barely had time to brace my legs and catch her in my arms. She broke apart against my chest, tears soaking my shirt.

"You're here," she sobbed.

I wrapped my arms around her and clutched her to my chest. My teeth clamped together in a vise grip, my throat screaming in pain as I held back my own tears, but I didn't know if I was hurting for her or Joe.

"I'll go see if there's some coffee," Rachel said and ducked out of the room.

When Eva's sobs turned to a light sniffle, she

blinked up at me, and her muscles tensed. Her palms pressed against my chest, and she pushed out of my embrace.

"No," she said, fresh tears dripping down her cheeks. "We can't...this isn't right. Is it?"

Her round hazel eyes looked at me as if I had some magical answer to our messed-up conundrum, so I parroted what my sister had said to me.

"We can be here for him and still be mad at him," I said. "This isn't black and white. It's a fucked-up gray, and we're allowed to live in it."

Eva sucked down a shuddering breath and nodded, tucking herself back into my arms.

"This feels good," she whispered, and I held her firmly, warmth seeping into my chest, blanketing the guilt that crept in. "It seems wrong," she said into my shirt, her breath hot and moist through the fabric, but she didn't move.

"We love him, and we want him to get better." I spoke against her temple, breathing in the fruity scent of her shampoo. "Let's focus on that."

I said it for her sake as much as mine because the feeling of her against me was sending all sorts of mixed signals ricocheting around my body.

Eva and I stayed like that, huddled together, leaching each other's solace, for minutes or hours, I didn't know. At some point, I loosened my grip, worried I'd held on too long, but she dug her fingers into my back and burrowed into the crook of my neck, not letting me go.

An overwhelming rush of love slammed through me like tiny bombs going off in every cell. I tried to stop it, but the searing ache in my gut exploded into my heart.

*Fuuuuuck.*

This was bad. This was very, very bad.

# Chapter 22

## *Eva*

Ethan's arms were a comforting balm, but none of this was real. Ethan and I were like a square peg in round hole, and nothing fit but everything made sense.

That unseen force that lived inside me and directed my emotions screamed at me when I pulled myself from Ethan's embrace. That fluttering feeling made me want to stay wrapped up in him and suck on the nectar he offered. It was big and scary and felt a lot like something that I shouldn't be feeling for Joe's best friend.

A shiver hit me when I stepped back from Ethan, but I dug my nails into my palms and made myself look at Joe.

That was my husband. For better or worse.

And maybe he wouldn't be my husband forever, but he was right now, and he was unconscious in a hospital bed. My heart didn't turn off just because he did a horrible, awful thing.

"I have to call his mom," I said, not looking at Ethan, and walked out of the room.

In the hallway, I pressed his mother's number. After several rings, it went to voice mail. I texted her to call me and then tried his dad. On the third ring, he picked up.

I told him the situation, and as expected, he was confused, then shocked, and then went into action. He said he and Tiffany would start driving down from Syracuse and be there by morning.

Joe was tight with his family. It was one of the things that solidified my choice to marry him. He came from a family that was filled with love and loyalty.

So why did he throw it all away? What did I do to make him cheat?

Yeah. Yeah. It wasn't my fault. I knew that. But I didn't really know that. Not in my heart.

There must be something that changed to make him go from being madly in love with me to having a full-on affair.

Ashley and Joe weren't some drunken mistake—a kiss in a bar, a lustful night of sex that he regretted in the morning. I could forgive that.

We would've had to work through it, but a mistake or a bad choice is one thing. Sneaking behind my back and lying to me daily was another. It felt personal and jagged.

I turned back to the room, but I couldn't face Joe in

that bed. I didn't know how to be the rock for him right now.

For the next thirty minutes, I walked the empty halls, but when one of the nurses looked at me suspiciously, I made my way back to the room.

"There you are," Rachel said, two Styrofoam cups in her hand, steam wafting off the top.

"Have you gone back to the room?" I asked.

"Yeah," she said. "Ethan and Ashley are still there."

"Were they talking?" I asked, curious what they'd say to each other.

"No. Ethan was on the sofa on his phone and Ashley was next to Joe in a chair."

I slumped against the wall. "I don't know if I can do this."

"Then don't. You don't have to be the one to care for him. Let Ashley get a neck cramp sitting in that chair. There's an empty room open next to Joe's. Lie down there for a bit."

I opened my mouth to protest, but I suddenly realized I didn't care. I knew I should care. I should rip Ashley away from his bedside, scream at her, and hurt her the way she was hurting me, but all I wanted to do was sleep and escape this purgatory that was my life.

"Okay." I relented and followed Rachel into the room. We kept the light off so we wouldn't draw attention, and I curled up in bed. "You don't need to stay. I know you have work early."

Rachel smiled softly and pulled the blanket over my arms. "I'll stay until you fall asleep. I'd stay all night but my comanager is out of town and I'm the only one who can open the studio."

I could hear the whir of the machines in Joe's room, doors opening and closing, announcements down the hall, and then I heard nothing.

\* \* \*

I woke up in the dark, confused. I gasped when I realized I was in a hospital room, forgetting I wasn't the patient.

I flung my feet to the side of the bed but stopped when a rush of dizziness hit me. Behind me, the sofa was empty; Rachel was gone. I breathed in and took a moment to remember the events from a few hours ago.

My phone screen said it was four, and there were several missed texts. Two were from Joe's parents. They'd arrive in a couple of hours. Rachel texted that she'd be back once her morning classes were done. The final text was from Ethan. He'd checked on me twice and sent a GIF of a bulldog asleep, drool on its jowls.

I swiped my mouth, but it was dry. I smiled. He was messing with me.

In the small bathroom, I splashed water on my face and rinsed out my mouth. My stomach rumbled, and I found a clementine in my purse. I usually kept a variety of food in my bag for when I needed a snack and didn't want to pay eight dollars for a coffee shop pastry.

I texted Ethan, *I don't drool.*

Immediately he sent a GIF of Anna from *Frozen* sleeping with her hair mussed and drooling.

*Shut up*, I texted and laughed, walking next door to Joe's room in search of Ethan.

The door was open. Ashley was bent over Joe blocking him from my view, but his legs shifted in the bed, and I squeaked in surprise. He was awake.

I stepped just past the threshold into the room, excitement rushing over me, but Ashley shifted, and I froze. They were kissing.

"I was so worried," Ashley whispered. "I love you, Joseph Patell. I don't ever want to lose you, baby."

I stumbled backward, my hand gripping the doorframe, keeping me upright as a ripple of shock crashed into me.

"I love you too, babe," Joe said and pulled Ashley back to his lips.

My mind spun, and I tried to calm my panic, afraid I would pass out.

*I love you too, babe.*

How many times had I heard those same words in that same tone from him? Hundreds?

I whirled out of the room, the floor shifting under my feet as I ran away.

"What's the matter? Is Joe— Did something happen?" Ethan was down the hall and rushed toward me, his face covered in fear, but the worry faded as soon as he met my turbulent gaze.

Ethan zipped past me and glanced into the room.

"Fuck," he said, walking back to me.

"I knew they were together. I knew they were fucking. But...*I love you*?" My hands fisted in front of me, wanting to hit something, to fight something, to tear this poison out of me. "He said I love you. To *her*. Her!"

Ethan cupped my elbow and pulled me into the empty room where I'd slept.

"What happened?" Ethan asked, his voice lowered, encouraging me to do the same.

"That's more than an affair." I walked back and forth, my breathing hurried like I'd run up a flight of stairs. "*I love you* isn't just fucking. It's time and energy and commitment. Why did he ask me to marry him if he was going to turn around and give his heart to that bitch?"

I yelled the last part, and Ethan glanced at the closed door, but no one came.

"Why didn't he tell me if he was unhappy? Why did he let it get so far?"

"I don't know," Ethan said softly. "I could kill him for breaking your heart."

My anger moved forward and pushed the pain aside. I slammed the heels of my palms into my eyes and screamed with my lips clamped shut.

"Hold on," Ethan said. Something soft pressed against my arm. "Scream into this." He handed me a pillow.

I hesitated a moment, then I shoved it against my face and screamed. I screamed until I sank to the floor, sobbing. His hand rubbed my upper back, and I swung my elbow, knocking Ethan to the ground.

"I don't want your pity," I snarled, lashing out at Ethan because of my anger at Joe.

"What do you want?" Ethan asked calmly. "Do you want to work it out with Joe?"

"No. I would've dumped him at the wedding, but I wasn't going to let him wreck what I'd built, what I'm still building. I keep thinking this will be over soon. But it feels like I'm going to be in this nightmare for the rest of my life. I hate feeling like this. So out of control."

"Then take control," Ethan said, kneeling in front of me. "Tell him you know. You can still get everything you want. I'll make sure Joe plays the part of the good husband until you get your citizenship. Then you can divorce, he can go live the rest of his boring life with Ashley, and you can be free."

"He won't play along," I challenged, my eyes wet but my tears gone.

"I'll make him," Ethan said, resolve thick in his voice.

"Why do you care?" I asked.

"Because what he did to you is wrong," Ethan said, something entering his eyes that stirred a warmth in my heart.

"You sent the car for us tonight, didn't you?" I asked.

Ethan hesitated. "Yes."

"Why?" I challenged, confused. "I spent the last week staring at my phone waiting for you to text or call.

I didn't need anything big, just something acknowledging that fooling around with me left some kind of impression." My voice cracked. "The worst thing in the world is to be forgotten."

"Fuck, I'm sorry, Evelyn. I'm so sorry. You know my dad came and then—I'm sorry. It's no excuse."

A sharp pain pressed into my heart.

"I'm an idiot. Forgive me?" Ethan opened his arms, and I stepped into them, resting my forehead against his chest.

It felt natural and right, wrapped in this little cocoon away from the rest of the world.

"My dad used to leave," I said.

Ethan's arms tensed around me.

"Mom and I would wake up and he'd be gone. No note. No calls. Mom would fix me breakfast and send me off to school like nothing was wrong. I'd look out the window after school as if he'd suddenly appear. This would go on for days, sometimes weeks, and then he'd walk in the door as if nothing happened." Ethan's heart pumped against my cheek, and I relaxed into the security of the steady timpani.

"I used to pull out my eyebrows from stress while Mom cleaned the house from top to bottom."

I paused, my chin trembling.

"It became a ritual. He'd leave, we'd create a temple, then he'd return, and nothing was spoken about it. Until the last time, when he never came back."

Ethan's thumb rubbed my back gently.

"I can't take it," I whispered into his chest, too

quiet for him to hear.

He peeled me off him and stared into my eyes. "Take what?"

My breath caught. He'd heard me.

"Being abandoned again."

He snatched me back to his chest, his biceps a vise around my shoulders.

"I'm so sorry," he said.

I bent my head back and pressed up on my toes, kissing him lightly. A thank-you.

Ethan cradled my face with his palms, tenderness in his light gaze.

"Evelyn." He swallowed. "I—"

"Fuck me," I blurted.

This was getting too real. We'd navigated so far from our original goal we were floating in the middle of the sea without a raft.

I'd had enough of thinking about Joe and feeling like shit.

"I want you to flip me over and pump me with your massive cock until the world falls away." I slid my hands over the coarse material covering his ass and tugged his pelvis against mine. "You're hard."

A thrill ran over my skin and landed between my legs.

"You just asked me to fuck you." His breathing was jagged. "My cock tends to respond to that. Are you sure—"

My lips pressed against his, stopping him. "Shut up and fuck me."

# Chapter 23

## *Ethan*

When had I developed a savior complex? I really needed to shut that down. Eva didn't need saving. She needed a distraction.

My right hand grazed Eva's cheek, my fingers cradling her chin, eager to fulfill her desires, but a jagged pain ran just beneath my arousal, stabbing me in the ribs.

I wanted more from Eva.

But I wasn't going to say no to her. Not when she was climbing up my body, begging to be fucked.

If this was what she needed, I was going to fuck her until Joe and her father and my stupid mistake were wiped from her brain and she was screaming into the pillow for an entirely different reason.

I hooked my finger under her chin, tugged her forward, and rocked my head from side to side, brushing my lips against hers.

Brooke Stanton

She trembled. I locked my arms around her ribs and I hugged her to me, lifting her up, her toes leaving the ground as I kissed her fully on the lips.

Mmmm...she felt so damn good.

In the past when I'd jerked off, it was always a face-less woman in my mind. But lately, my fantasies were consumed by Eva, and I blew my load the moment my hand hit my cock like I was a fourteen-year-old boy.

My dick twitched in my jeans, and I relaxed against the hospital bed, willing myself to last and enjoy every sweet moment with her.

"I want to be lost in you," Eva said, her fingers raking up the back of my neck and digging into the hair at the base of my scalp.

She drew my head to her, and her tongue flicked out and licked my bottom lip. I groaned and opened for her, our tongues sliding together in a sultry dance.

I bent my knees and scooped her up, her legs wrapping around me. The kisses turned from soft and warm to fierce and scorching. Our mouths ravaged each other, and she clenched my body tight against her. Her small breasts smashed into my chest, her fingers dug into my scalp, and her pelvis pressed into my stomach.

"You're amazing, baby," I panted between kisses.

She wore leggings, and I could feel her heat against my belly through the thin material.

Eva's hands slid down my back, a fever following where she caressed. She wrenched my shirt out of my pants and shoved her hands down the back of my jeans, her fingers digging into the mound of my ass.

I grumbled. My cock was a steel rod, trapped. As if she sensed my discomfort, she pulled her hands out and sank to her knees in front of the bulge in my pants.

One moment she was a frisky koala wrapped around me and the next she was kneeling in front of me, unbuttoning my jeans and shoving them to my ankles.

I shivered with relief as the cool air hit my cock.

"I want to be inside you," I growled.

"Shh." Her gaze raked up my body and she smiled wryly, her lids heavy with lust. "It's called foreplay."

I laughed but clamped my lips shut when she blew moist air against the tip of my cock. My balls tightened, and I forced my hands to grip the mattress behind me to prevent me from grabbing Eva's face and forcing her mouth on my cock.

She stuck her tongue out and licked the drop of pre-cum from my slit.

"Your cock is beautiful," she said and brushed her lips over my tip.

She looked at my dick like it was a piece of cake she couldn't wait to feast upon.

*Oh fuck.* My balls drew further into my groin, aching.

Eva opened her lips, a cavern ready to be filled, but she paused.

"Evelyn, if you don't suck me, I'm gonna need to take care of this. Like right fucking now," I groaned, my balls throbbing. Why did she always tease me?

"Patience, grasshopper."

Hell, if this little game stopped her tears and gave her pleasure, I'd stand here all fucking day.

Eva lifted the hem of my shirt where it rested on the top of my dick, and she wrapped her sweet mouth around my cock. My hips jerked, and I released a long trembling sigh.

Her tongue wet the shaft and she moved down, taking me fully into her mouth.

"Oh fuck!" I roared, falling forward, catching myself with my hands on her shoulders.

My legs shook as my tip hit the back of her throat and she sucked me like a Hoover.

"Holy shit, Evelyn." I gritted my teeth, willing myself not to come. Her tongue circled my tip, and she tucked in her lips and slid down my shaft, her right hand gripping my balls and tugging them gently.

"Wait!" I shoved her off, nearly exploding all over her face. I took several deep breaths, trying to gain control.

My palms rolled over her shoulders and down her slight biceps, and I lifted her until she stood in front of me, her lips puffy, her eyelids hooded, and her pupils large. I could almost smell the pheromones wafting off her.

In a quick movement, I twisted her around and pressed her belly against the thin mattress. I dropped to my knees on the cool tile floors, yanked her leggings and panties off, and threw them across the room.

My hands clasped the bulbs of her ass, and I spread

them apart. Saliva filled my mouth at the sight of her wet pink lips.

She whimpered against the sheets where she half lay. I leaned forward and mimicked what she'd done to me as I breathed out a stream of warm air over her glistening pussy.

"Is this okay?" I asked, needing to hear her consent before I pillaged her, because once I started, it would be a Herculean effort to stop.

"Yes," she mewled, her voice barely audible. "Please."

I stuck my tongue out and licked her from clit to anus. She trembled under my mouth, and my cock twitched where it stood at full mast between my legs.

I spread her ass cheeks wider and tilted my head until I had the perfect angle, then sucked her clit into my mouth. She tasted sweet and ripe for the taking. She moaned loudly, and a shiver of excitement ran across my skin.

*Damn.* The sounds of her pleasure were mind-altering, and I was desperate for more. I released her swollen bud and plunged my tongue between her slit and she gasped.

I rocked back on my toes, my teeth grazing her thigh as my fingers replaced my mouth and sank into her hot chamber. At the same time, I swiped my thumb over her swollen nub, and her hips rolled against my hand, encouraging me.

The small muscles inside her pussy gripped my

fingers, and I worked my thumb firmly against the apex of her mound.

"Oh God, that's so hot," she murmured.

Eva twisted her head and swung her lustful gaze at me. "I want your cock, baby. I want it now."

She didn't have to ask twice.

I used my legs to push to a stand, my stiff cock rubbing the backs of her silky legs. I wrapped my palm around my shaft and slid my cock from side to side over her ass cheeks.

"I want you so bad," she said, her voice almost a sob.

Then I remembered. "Oh shit."

"What?" she said, craning her neck to look at me.

I lay, my chest against her back, and whispered in her ear, my fingers playing with her clit as I said, "I don't have protection. But I'll take care of you, baby."

She reached behind her and grabbed my bare ass, pressing my hips against her from behind, my cock rubbing her anus.

*Fuck.* Why didn't I have a condom?

"Are you clean?" she asked.

"I get tested every six weeks when I'm dating, but I haven't fucked anyone in months," I said.

"I'm on the pill, and after I discovered Joe was cheating, I got tested immediately." Her nails dug into the thick muscles of my backside. "The bastard didn't give me anything."

She dipped her hand between my thighs, finding my cock.

"Evelyn," I groaned, my jaw tightening around her name.

I took her hand off my dick, and glided her arm above her head, then clasped her other hand and pinned them together, her face in the mattress.

With my free hand, I rounded her hip and dipped my fingers into her, wetting them, then slid them out and massaged her clit.

"I'm gonna fuck you so hard, baby."

"Do it, Ethan." She squirmed. "Fill me up."

But I didn't give it to her. Not yet.

"I want you on the brink," I whispered in her ear.

"I am," she whimpered helplessly.

I took my fingers out of her pussy and wet my cock with her juices, angling my tip in front of her slit.

With a gentle nudge, I pressed against her opening, her lips widening over my tip.

"It's not enough." She pressed back suddenly, her pussy spreading over my cock, her hips slamming back until I was fully engulfed in her.

"Oh fuck, baby." A shock of pleasure blasted into my dick buried inside her. "You're so damn tight."

"You're so damn big," she gasped.

I shifted my pelvis back an inch, then pushed forward, slower this time, sinking myself easily into her wet folds, stretching her.

I breathed out a shaky breath, holding on to every bit of willpower so I didn't come.

Eva's pussy tightened around my dick, and I pulled out quickly.

"Wait, baby," I said, looking at my cock, which was shiny from her sap. "Your pussy is so good, but I want to wait for you."

"I can't hold on either, Ethan. Fuck me hard."

I snatched the pillow next to her and shoved it under her head.

"You're gonna need this, baby."

I didn't go gently into her night. I slammed my dick inside her cavern, falling over her and biting her shoulder, as the little muscles on her neck flexed.

"Rougher," she panted.

Jesus. My heart pounded wildly, my cock slip-sliding in her juices, her walls as tight as a Chinese finger trap. My right hand reached around and played her clit like a world-class guitarist, my balls slapping her ass with every thrust.

"Yes. Oh God, I'm right there," she panted into the pillow.

I quickened my fingers and backed her ass further against me.

Oh, shit, this was glorious. She was perfection.

I rolled my hips, my balls tightening, grinding down on her, my cock a fucking steel rod.

"I'm coming, Ethan," she cried, her muscles pulsing around my cock. "Oh yes. I'm coming so hard."

She screamed and twisted her face into the pillow, her body quivering as her orgasm wracked her body.

"Oh fuck, Eva. Yes, baby!" My orgasm ripped through me, our slick bodies quaking against each other as we reached our euphoria together, my face buried in the curve of her neck, sucking her salty skin.

I lapped it up, her pussy milking my cock, clenching and unclenching as she rode her orgasmic wave. My chest constricted, my balls erupted, and my heart broke free of all restraints. I shoved her shirt up her back and rested my chest there, needing to remove all barriers and be as close to her as possible.

I sank to the floor, taking Eva with me, cradling her fiercely against my body. The rush of affection that overtook me was so powerful, tears pricked my eyes.

I placed a soft kiss against her shoulder blade. She reached back with her hand and tugged me closer to her, but if I lay there another moment, I might say something really stupid.

A movement across the room caught my attention, and I jerked my head toward the door.

Ashley stood there, her mouth gaping.

I swallowed a yelp and quickly looked beside me, but Eva lay with her back to the door.

The look of shock melted from Ashley's face and was replaced by something else. I expected satisfaction or smugness, but it was relief.

I gathered my clothes and yanked them on. Ashley slinked out of the room but I couldn't risk her saying anything to Joe.

"I'll be right back, baby," I whispered in Eva's ear, and she grunted, already half-asleep, but I never returned.

# Chapter 24

## *Eva*

I think I went momentarily insane. Two weeks had passed since Ethan and I slept together in the hospital. My belly contracted and released as it always did when I remembered. I'd been filled with courage and determination that night, but it seeped out the moment I'd woken up on that cold hospital floor, Ethan gone.

I hadn't seen him since, and the more time passed, the more it felt like a wet dream instead of reality.

Ethan had texted and sent funny GIFs but nothing of meaning. I could've sworn things had shifted between us that night, but nope. We were back to where we were before Joe's accident.

Politely indifferent.

I slumped against my seat, wrapped in remorse.

"Are you thinking about Ethan?" Rachel asked from the train seat next to me.

"No," I quickly answered, heat cresting my neck

and cheeks. I ducked my head sheepishly and said, "Yes."

The train sped along the tracks, shooting us upstate to Hamperville, Joe and Ethan's hometown outside of Syracuse.

I'd only been to Joe's parents' home a few times. He'd been shy about taking me there because they lived in a trailer park.

I didn't have much experience with trailer parks, just the stereotypical images I saw in movies or TV or driving past them on a highway, but his parents' trailer park was nothing like the run-down, depressing place I'd imagined.

It was bright and clean with green grass, flowerbeds, and freshly painted siding. Neighbors walked around with smiles on their faces, chatting with each other or sitting out front on a lawn chair enjoying a peaceful day. The people that lived there took pride in their community, and it showed.

"You're sure Ethan's going to be there?" Rachel asked, fiddling with one of the many holes in her white jeans.

"Of course. Ethan's like family to the Patells."

Since the accident, Joe'd been staying at his parents' home. He needed to be monitored twenty-four hours a day at first, and I couldn't do it with my job. I asked his mother to stay with us and help, but she suggested he come back home until his doctor cleared him to go to work so she could split the task with Joe's father.

I'd been relieved. I hadn't trusted myself not to strangle Joe in his sleep if I was left alone with him. Even after he'd nearly died.

I was haunted by Ashley and Joe's declaration in that hospital room, and it was all mixed up with sleeping with Ethan.

There was also this annoying swirling feeling low in my belly that crept up to my heart when I wasn't paying attention.

"Did you call Ethan?" Rachel asked.

"No."

Rachel raised an eyebrow. "So you can't be mad at him."

"I'm not!" I huffed. "But his texts were perfunctory, mostly about Joe's recovery, so I kept mine short too."

"And he ran out after you guys..." Rachel made a circle with her left hand and poked her right index finger into the hole several times.

I batted her hands apart. "I was still in my orgasmic haze when he yanked his clothes on and rushed out the door."

Rachel sucked her teeth. "Yeah. That doesn't sound good."

"Told ya." I glared out the window. It was a sunny Saturday morning, but inside all I felt was doom and gloom.

Joe was going back to work on Monday and moving back into our place today. His parents had invited his closest friends over to send him off on a high note.

I'd visited him twice over the past couple of weeks. It was a five-hour train ride from the city, and I had work and I really didn't want to be with him and his family.

His mom and dad were awesome, and I loved being in the happy cocoon of their family, but Joe had turned everything rotten.

"How was the last visit?" Rachel asked.

"Fine. Joe was nearly fully recovered last week, but the doctor wanted to wait another week before he climbed up ladders and worked on roofs." I shrugged. "A precaution."

"Has Ashley visited?" Rachel said.

"I don't want to know."

What I didn't say was that my mind had been clogged by Ethan. Reliving the way he'd touched me, the words he'd said, and the way his cock stretched me like I was a fucking flower he was pollinating. My sex clenched every time I thought of him, wanting more, scared that he thought I was messed up for asking him to fuck me while my husband lay in a hospital bed.

"You did nothing wrong." Rachel snapped the exposed bra strap on my shoulder.

"Hey!" I said, rubbing my skin where it stung. "How did everything get so confusing?"

"Your husband started banging his ex-girlfriend as soon as you got married." Rachel lifted my bra strap again in warning.

"Don't you dare." I batted her hand off.

I blew a strand of lavender hair off my face. Rachel

convinced me to use a color shampoo to get me out of my slump. I had to admit I looked kind of awesome, and it made me feel a little bit like I was playing someone else for the day.

"Remember who the assholes are here." Rachel looked pointedly at me, then went back to reading her Manga book on her phone.

\* \* \*

An Uber dropped us in front of the Patells' trailer. It was a cream-paneled double-wide with large shrubs and rows of petunias bordering the front.

It was furnished by Wayfair and garage sales, but it was well put together with bright colors and fun patterns. His mother had an eye for design, just not the money to buy expensive furnishings.

They'd set up their coal barbecue in the backyard, and the neighbors had brought over folding tables and chairs and set them up. It was a potluck. I brought a family-size Stouffer's lasagna, and I'd made Joe his favorite thumbprint cookies which I usually made him at Christmastime.

Rachel was helping Joe's father, Luis, cook the hot dogs and set out the condiments. I was on a small ladder hanging string lights I'd brought from home. I'd bought them a year ago, thinking I'd hang them in our bedroom for ambiance, but Joe hated them. They'd been stuffed in the back of a drawer until now.

"Come into the kitchen when you're done," Joe's mom, Tiffany, said.

The kitchen was small, and a cart on rollers with a butcher-block top served as extra counter space. I pulled it over to cut tomatoes and cucumber for a salad.

"Joe will be back from the store soon, and I wanted to talk to you before he got here."

My hand faltered and a piece of cucumber went flying to the floor.

"Why don't you put the knife down," Tiffany said, gently placing her hand on my arm.

I kept my eyes down, the bubble of anxiety pressing painfully inside my chest.

"Honey, look at me." She spoke in her tender, motherly tone.

My chin wobbled, and I gripped the edge of the cart, staring at the thin linoleum floor. To my horror, tears crested behind my eyelids.

I feared if I spoke, I'd tell her everything.

"I'm not going to ask what's going on between Joe and you because that's your business, but I'm here if you need to talk. I know I'm his mother, but that doesn't mean I think the sun shines out of his ass."

A laugh popped out of me, but I kept my gaze down, afraid to trust her words. She set a large, wooden bowl on the cart next to the chopped vegetables and stayed beside me.

"I know he can be selfish, and marriages take work, but you've only been married a few months and you seem miserable."

A looked at her sideways, trying to discern if she was blaming me, but her eyes were soft. My lips trembled, on the verge of telling her everything, but the front door swung open, and I clamped my mouth shut, swiping at my tears.

Ethan walked in, Ashley by his side, smiling and bouncy, a bouquet of daisies in her hands.

I gasped and whipped around, facing the kitchen wall. The coil of anxiety strangled my gut as questions zipped through my head. Why was Ethan with Ashley? Why was she smiling? Had the guilt over what we'd done caused him to rush into the enemy's arms?

Tiffany greeted them, and Ashley gave her the bouquet. I threw vegetables into the bowl so hard that several of them flew out.

"We brought a case of Coors, Tiff," Ashley said, and my hand halted. *We?*

"You can put it in the cooler outside," Tiffany said, opening the back door.

Ethan walked into the kitchen area, his arms heavy with the beer case, and stopped right next to me. I knew it was weird that I hadn't turned to say hello, but I was paralyzed.

"Did you pass Joe on the way here?" Tiffany asked.

"He's outside parking the car," Ethan said.

I tossed the lettuce in the salad and doused it with the salad dressing. I stepped around Ethan and backed into the door to the backyard, pressing it open.

"Evelyn." Ethan put his hand on my arm, stopping

me from exiting. He lowered his voice. "We need to talk."

I cut a sharp glance at him, furious. He had two weeks to explain why he D. B. Coopered me. I didn't want to hear it in front of all these people.

I yanked my arm out of his grip, pushed the door fully open, and walked down the few steps.

"Eva, we—"

I kicked the door shut and cut off Ethan's words.

After dumping the salad on the table, I walked past the trailer into the neighbor's yard, my belly aching so much I feared I'd hurl.

"Eva?" Rachel came up behind me. "What happened?"

"It's Ethan. He showed up with Ashley literally on his arm."

"Did you ask him why?" Rachel asked.

"I'm done with him," I huffed.

"This is fucking ridiculous. You two have to talk." She turned to the yard and yelled, "Ethan!"

I snatched her arm and hissed, "What the hell are you doing?"

"Stopping this bullshit. Ethan's no saint, but he wouldn't be chummy with Ashley unless he had an ulterior motive. Ethan! Get your ass over here," Rachel hollered.

He walked out of the trailer, his hands shoved in his pockets. He wore another classic Ethan shirt—a navy, short-sleeve, button-down with polar bears in sunglasses all over it.

But when he got closer, I took my first real look at him. His clothes were wrinkled, and before he slid his sunglasses over his eyes, I saw they were bloodshot. His hair was greasy and mussed, but on him, it looked sexy.

"What the hell's wrong with you? Why did you bring that dingleberry?" Rachel asked and punched his arm.

"Hey," Ethan said, rubbing his bicep.

"I didn't bring her. We were on the same train."

"You took a train?" I asked, raising an eyebrow. "You have a fleet of drivers and a plane."

Ethan shifted toward me and my heart beat faster, clouding my brain, but I forced myself to focus.

"I have a car service and a co-op jet I share," Ethan corrected. "A train was more practical for this trip. And more environmental."

"You're a jerk," I blurted.

He slid the glasses down his nose and looked at me over the top of them. My heart seized in my chest.

"Excuse me?" he said.

"I told you all that stuff about my dad and then you ran away. I wasn't asking for much, but ignoring me afterward was shitty."

"I didn't run away," he thundered. "I had something I had to do."

"And you remembered it the moment you finished sticking your dick in me?" I hissed.

"No!" Ethan's hands flew up. Ashley was watching us with eagle eyes, but we were too far away for her to hear anything. "It...it was something urgent."

214

I didn't believe him. Nothing could have pulled me away. I could've stayed on that hard, cold tile floor with Ethan for hours.

"So you're done with this affair thing?" I asked.

"No," he said, his voice hard. "Are you done?"

"No," I shot back.

"Good."

We glared at each other, obviously *not* good, and then he turned and strode away.

"That went well," Rachel said, and I shoved her. She caught my arm and pulled me into a sideways hug. "I still love ya."

"I know. Too bad you don't have a dick."

"Strap-on?" she deadpanned.

I laughed, but when I looked across the yard, all humor faded. Ethan was holding Ashley's hand, showing her something on his phone and speaking softly into her ear.

"I'm sure it's nothing," Rachel said, following my glare.

But I wasn't sure of anything.

# Chapter 25

## *Ethan*

Eva sat at one of the long worktables at Dreamary, typing rapidly on her computer. The lavender coloring had faded from her hair, and it was almost back to honey blonde.

My feet wanted to walk to her, my hands wanted to touch her, my nose to smell her, my body to do way more, but I held firm to my spot. I wasn't here for her.

"Thanks for this, Ethan." Enzo, the producer of the podcast *Do Good*, greeted me with a fist bump.

He contacted me this morning to fill in for a last-second guest spot to talk about my foundation. They particularly liked the angle of the young techie who sold his company for millions and turned around and put most of that money into a nonprofit to help underprivileged kids instead of buying boats and luxury cars and basically being a wanker.

I had no idea if Eva knew I was asked to do the podcast. It had been several weeks since the barbecue, and I'd barely seen her. Everything had gotten so twisted since the hospital.

After Ashley saw us, I chased after her and cornered her. I'd told her if she breathed a word of what she'd seen to Joe, I'd write scathing reviews on all the sites where her veterinary practice was listed.

To drive my point in deeper, I'd pulled her aside at the barbecue and showed her mock-ups of the reviews on my phone. I threatened to post them and reminded her I was a programmer. I knew how to get those reviews to the top of the list.

By focusing on damage control with Ashley, I may have fucked it up with Eva. I hadn't completely ignored her, but I'd been so distracted by Ashley, work, and these new scary emotions living inside me, I'd kept communication to the minimum.

The whole revenge affair had been a mistake.

I wanted to be with Eva, pure and unfettered, not because she was in a world of pain and wanted to punish Joe.

Sweat broke out on my back as I watched her. Her nails dug into her neck, scratching roughly, a sign she was stressed. Was it about me? Joe? Work?

We needed to have a conversation.

Just not right now.

I followed Enzo to a small podcast studio with an oval table in the center and several microphones on stands. This was a pre-interview. If it went well, I'd be back tomorrow to record the podcast.

An hour later, Enzo thanked me and walked out,

leaving me alone in the studio to find my way out. It had been easy talking about my foundation. When you're passionate about something, it usually is.

Every fiber of me ached to see Eva, but I needed to leave her alone. Her life was too complicated to add my confused feelings into the mix.

I closed my eyes and gripped the leather chair in front of me until the urge passed.

When I opened my eyes, Eva was on the other side of the window from the studio, her head bent over her phone, looking distressed.

"Eva," I said, stepping outside the door.

"Oh." She glanced up. startled.

The citrus scent of her shampoo wafted under my nose, and I shoved my hands in my pockets.

"I forgot you were coming today." Her eyes traveled back to her phone. She clicked the side button and then shoved it into her back pocket.

"Dammit," she said, tears pricking her eyes. She swiped them away.

"Eva, what's wrong?" I asked, alarmed.

"Rachel's on a cruise ship for two weeks teaching Pilates," Eva ground out, her voice thick.

"Is she okay?" I asked.

"What? Oh, yeah. I just need her. The prosecutor emailed me that I have to testify tomorrow," she said. "I really don't want to."

Her chin quivered, and the pull to comfort her was so strong it hurt.

"I know we're not friends, but..." Her voice faltered.

I closed the gap between us and folded her in my arms. God, it was like a hole inside me had been filled when she sank into me.

She looked up at me, her hazel eyes shiny. "I feel stupid. I don't know why I'm so upset."

"Against the kid who stole your phone?" I asked, and she nodded.

She went into the studio where it was quiet and sank to the floor, crossing her legs and dropping her forehead in her hands.

I sat across from her and touched her knee, drawing her attention to me. "Why are you worried?"

"The prosecutor said the judge was hearing his case tomorrow and I have to be a witness. I don't want to ruin the kid's life. He's only thirteen. It's too young." She breathed out shakily.

"What do you have to testify about?" I asked, squeezing her knee.

"I have to point him out as the one who stole my phone." She looked up at the padded ceiling and shook her head. "Maybe I can lie and say I don't remember."

"You can't lie," I said. "It's perjury."

An idea popped into my head, and I pulled my phone from my pants, typing in the search bar.

"Has the prosecutor said anything about making a deal for the kid or anything?" I asked, navigating my results.

"Not to me."

I stood up, typing quickly on my phone.

"Send me the details, and I'll be there tomorrow." I bent forward and quickly hugged her. There was a questioning look on her face but I had no time to explain. "You won't be alone."

# Chapter 26

## *Eva*

I stared at my computer but didn't see any of the words of the email I'd been typing a response to on the screen. The prosecutor had just called, and I was in a daze.

I didn't have to testify today.

I'd been up half the night stressing about it, but Sherry, the prosecutor, said the public defender presented her office with a deal late last night and the judge agreed to the terms that morning.

Instead of going to juvenile detention, the kid, Amir, agreed to do community service with a guardian for the state. I didn't ask for details. I didn't care!

The lead anchor that had been on my shoulders lifted as soon as it was clear Amir wouldn't be going to detention.

I laughed, the relief rushing over me again. Yeah, he'd stolen my phone, but I doubted going to jail would be a wake-up call for the boy.

Across the office, Ethan walked with determination down the side of the long communal worktables, following Enzo. Ethan's stride was long, and he wore skinny navy pants that hugged his lean legs and a graphic tee with a picture of baby Yoda. His gaze drifted to me, but he didn't stop, only offered a small wave.

My knees bounced but I spread my hands over them, resisting the urge to run and tell him the good news.

Since the hospital, a rippling giddy feeling had lived in my belly when I thought of Ethan. The comfort he'd offered yesterday had cooled my panic, and I'd almost called him last night and asked him to come over. Not for revenge sex. I only wanted him to be there with me. It was the only thing that could've steadied my nerves.

"Eva, come to my office." Derrick motioned me from his office doorway.

I walked to Derrick's office, taking a seat in a chair in front of his desk. He sat across from me, his hands worrying each other in his lap.

"Is everything okay?" I asked.

"You tell me." Derrick stared at me with his stern dark eyes and waited for an answer.

"Oh, uh..." I stumbled over a response, not expecting to be put on the spot by my boss. "I'm fine. I mean, I know I messed up that booking, but I promise it won't happen again."

I'd mis-scheduled the original guest for *Good Deeds*

and I'd needed to find a replacement fast. Ethan's foundation fit the podcast's messaging, so I gave Enzo his number, praying he could do it.

Ethan didn't know it, but he saved my ass when he agreed to the interview today.

"It's more than that. You're distracted. Ever since your wedding, it's like you're only half here, and it's affecting your work. You used to be the most efficient junior producer."

Heat crept up my neck. I wanted to argue, but after two decades on the police force, Derrick could detect a lie better than anyone I'd ever met.

Derrick was a good boss, understanding and compassionate. He was like a sage father but with no condescension.

That's why I decided to tell the truth.

"My husband's cheating on me," I said and continued quickly. "I found out right after the wedding, but I'm waiting to confront him until my citizenship goes through. I can't stay in the States or work for Dreamary without it. And despite my head being clouded these past two months, I love this job. I want to keep it. It's just been hard. I'm sorry. I'll do better. I promise."

Derrick steepled his fingers in front of his mouth, thinking.

"Do you want to work it out with your husband? I can suggest some counselors," Derrick said, his tone neutral.

"No. It's over."

"I thought you had a visa," Derrick said.

"It's expiring."

"Have you had the interview yet?" he asked.

"It's scheduled for the end of the month."

He nodded, his brow furrowed in concentration.

My phone beeped, and I glanced down as a notification appeared on the screen. I gasped.

"Is everything okay?" Derrick asked, leaning forward.

"Yeah," I said, an icy chill running over me. "Sorry. I...what were you saying?"

I looked at the image on the screen again and the chill turned to a burning heat.

"I'm sorry," I said again, standing on shaky legs. "I have to go. I...I have to take care of something."

"Eva, stop." He spoke with authority, and I halted. "Where are you going?"

"I...I don't know," I said, realizing I couldn't do anything about the images I just saw on the screen. Not yet.

"I think I can help you," Derrick said. "Sit."

I did as I was instructed. Derrick spoke, explaining how he could help my situation. As he did, my emotions shifted from shock to confusion to elation and finally to gratitude.

"You'd do that for me?" I asked, shaking my head back and forth, laughing through tears of relief.

"I'd be doing it for the company. I don't want to lose you. But"—he placed his hands flat on the desk and looked directly into my eyes—"you need to take some personal time. Things happen in our lives that are disruptive. I get it. But you need to handle it and not bring it into the office next time. I'm happy to give you personal leave when these things come up."

My phone beeped with another notification, and this time I knew exactly what I needed to do.

"I promise I'm going to take care of the mess of my life and come back focused and ready to work. Thank you again. I should've thought of this."

I rushed out but stopped next to the podcast studio where Ethan was recording. He had headphones on, his brown hair swept to the side, and he spoke enthusiastically into the mic. I rubbed my chest, which suddenly burned. My eyes swept over his straight nose and landed on his lips, and I swallowed over the pressure in my throat.

I shook my head, moving on.

Derrick had made it clear that he would help me, but only if I helped myself. And that's what I planned to do.

* * *

The subway ride uptown had been swift, and I was at my apartment within twenty minutes.

I paused outside the front door, listening to the noises coming from inside. Joe was meant to be at work.

My heart thundered as I wrapped my hand around

the handle of my apartment door, anticipating what I was going to find on the other side.

I pressed the door open slowly and gasped.

Across the room, Joe and Ashley lay on the couch. It took a moment for the image of their bodies tangled together to become clear. Joe lay on his back, his head toward the door. Ashley's ass was in the air facing me as she reversed-cowboyed him.

My body trembled, and I wished Ethan were with me. For a moment, I almost turned around and walked out. I knew this moment would come one day, but I didn't realize how shaken up I'd be.

I sucked a breath deep into my lungs. It was now or never.

I dropped my fob into the bowl loudly, and both their heads whipped toward me. Ashley yelped and clambered off Joe. She snatched her discarded vet jacket and covered her body.

Joe's face filled with surprise, but he made no move to cover his naked body.

He bent at the waist and looked down. "Fuck. You bent my dick."

Ashley ignored him, staring at me.

"I didn't think you liked to recycle," I said, my voice strangely calm.

"What?" Joe glanced up.

"Ashley's used goods." My smile was anything but sweet. "Couldn't find anything fresh?"

"Fuck you," Ashley said, hurrying to get dressed, but her hands shook, making her fumble.

A slimy layer of disgust covered me. Watching them in the raw act of sex shook me to the core. It was different from hearing them on the fire escape.

Revulsion coiled in my gut. It was an angry, throbbing, raw emotion, and something snapped in me. I leaped at Ashley and yanked her black hair.

"Ah!" she screamed, clawing at my hand, but I wrenched it at the roots and turned her head in an awkward twist.

"Let go of her!" Joe grabbed my shoulders and tugged me back. My calves hit the coffee table and my grip loosened and I fell sideways, catching myself with my free hand. My right hand was still tangled in Ashley's hair, and she fell on top of me.

Joe lifted her off and she huddled next to him, his arm around her protectively. Her eyes were two venomous slits as she glared at me.

I walked to the bedroom and slammed the door.

"I'm glad you found us," Joe shouted from the other room. "This joke of a marriage needed to end."

I reached under the bed, my hand finding what I was looking for, and I walked out, opened the plastic container, and threw the contents on them.

The little spiders.

Ashley screeched as if I'd set her on fire, shaking and swiping her body.

"You're fucking crazy," Joe said as he swatted at them. "What the hell are you even doing with these?"

He sneezed. I'd never fully gotten rid of all the cat dander.

"I've known about your affair for months, asshole. Why do you think there were spiders on the bed when you wanted to fuck me last month? Why did your cat allergies suddenly appear when we don't have a cat? Why are your clothes so tight?"

Realization dawned on him, and he lunged for me and dug his fingers into my shoulders. He held me tight, but he didn't hit me or hurt me in any other way. He just held me there, his fingers digging in.

"You're gonna pay for this, you frigid bitch. There's no way I'm going to any interview for you now. Your visa's gonna run out, you'll lose your job, and you'll go back to freezing Canada with your icy heart and pussy. I can't believe I ever loved you."

"You never loved me," I snarled. "Do you know how easy it was to manipulate you? You told Ethan you wanted to divorce me, but the minute I put doubt in your mind that Ashley would leave you if you did, you scurried away and wouldn't do it. And your clothes? You're such an idiot. I knew you'd go crazy when they stopped fitting. I've been playing you this whole time. I've known about the affair since our wedding day. I never had food poisoning. I just couldn't stand the thought of your dick anywhere near me."

Joe's face went from crimson to ivory, and his grip loosened on my shoulders with each new confession.

"The only reason I didn't kick you in the balls and dump your ass that day was because of my citizenship."

Joe dropped his hands, his face bewildered.

"You'll never get your citizenship now," he said, but there was less bite in his words.

"Maybe not. But torturing you these past few months has been worth the sacrifice."

Ashley shuffled to Joe and tugged him toward the front door.

"Come on, Joe. We'll deal with her later," she pleaded, her gaze swinging around, looking for the remaining spiders. They were tiny and harmless but very effective.

"I'll deal with her now," he said, his voice thunderous, his anger snapping back. "Get the hell out of this apartment. I'm breaking the lease, and you'll pay for any costs. Otherwise, I'm gonna tell your boss what a psycho you are. Not that it matters. You won't be allowed to work there anymore. You'll pay all the divorce fees, and if you try and get any money from me, I'll contact immigration and tell them it was a green card marriage and you'll never be allowed back here again. You could even go to jail."

Joe snatched his phone and keys and pulled Ashley to the door.

"I'll be back tomorrow, and I want your shit gone." Joe narrowed his gaze. "Or I'll make that call. I can play the revenge game too."

# Chapter 27

## *Ethan*

At first, I thought it was a mirage. Evelyn Hart was standing in my office next to Amir.

"What's he doing here?" she asked, her eyes wildly looking him up and down.

"I was going to tell you," I said, ushering her away from him.

The day Eva told me about testifying, I'd left and called the prosecutor's office and asked if they'd be open to Amir being under my guardianship and doing community work at my foundation.

They'd agreed. The prosecutor was tired of seeing these kids going into the system with no chance of redemption. As Sherry said, they just got smarter at not getting caught when they got out.

The judge and Sherry thought this arrangement would give Amir a better chance at not being a repeat offender. Especially since it was a minor offense.

"'S all good?" he asked, looking confused by Eva's reaction to him. "I didn't mean to scare the lady."

He must not have recognized Eva. I doubt he got a good look at her before he snatched her phone.

"We're fine," I said. "Can you shred that stack of paper next to the copier? Then go help Tyron with the coding pamphlets."

"Cool," he said.

"Are you okay?" I huddled next to Eva when he was gone. "I'm sorry I didn't say anything. I was waiting until—Eva, what's wrong?"

Her skirt was askew, her ponytail was lopsided with several strands hanging loose, and her eyes skittered around the open space.

"Yep." She smiled, but it looked like she was cringing. "Can we talk in your office?"

I walked her down the short hallway and into the office I'd claimed as my own. It had a small desk and bookshelves against one wall and a window behind the desk. Nothing fancy. I only came into the foundation offices a few times a month. Mostly I worked from home.

I gave the larger offices to the executives that ran the foundation on a daily basis. I didn't need all the pomp to fluff my ego. That's not why I started the foundation. I'd been hesitant to even rent this office space with its sleek furniture and modern fixtures, but my sister had convinced me.

Savi said the foundation was about making lives better and I didn't want my employees to be depressed because they had to go to work in a cramped, smelly, mildewy office every day—she'd been talking about the sad space I'd wanted to rent. It had been cheap and utilitarian at best.

Work was where people lived these days. Let them enjoy it, she'd said.

And she was right. It was bright and cheery, and I think it added to people's productivity.

All this fluttered through my mind as I watched Eva take in the small room.

"This is snug." She stepped forward, her breasts grazing my T-shirt. "I like it."

She fisted my shirt and tugged me close, her lips pressing against mine. She dragged her hand down my abs and popped the button on my trousers open.

"Whoa." I gently pushed her off.

Something was off.

"Hey, look at me," I said gently, tucking my finger under her chin. "What's going on, Eva?"

She pulled her chin away from my hand and I thought she was about to cry, but when she flicked her eyes up to mine, they were filled with steel.

"You're still with me on this, right?" she asked. "You want Joe and Ashley to pay for the shit they did."

I placed my hand on her cheek, my thumb caressing it. "I do," I said, drawing out the second word. "Is that why you're here? You want a revenge fuck? Because I don't want to do that anymore."

The pink in Eva's cheeks faded and she untangled herself from me, putting several inches between us.

"I thought you liked it," she said, her voice accusatory.

I looked at the cat clock with the moving tail and eyes on the wall behind her. It was a gift from my sister when I opened the office to remind me not to take myself too seriously.

"That's the problem, Eva." I sucked down a shaky breath. "I like it too much."

Her eyes lit up. "You do? So you're still with me?"

Her palms slid up my pecs and into my hair, pulling me back to her.

Damn, this woman was beautiful. Even disheveled and wild. My heart swelled, wanting to carry her out of there and into my bed. I wanted to trace every inch of her body and make love to her. Then I wanted to lie with her for hours as she told me about her childhood, her dreams, her fears, everything. I wanted to know every inch of her, inside and out.

"God yes, I'm with you," I said.

"I want you," she said, her lips feathering against mine. "I'm tired of all the fighting and revenge."

"I want you too, baby. So bad." My palms circled her cheeks, and I brought her face to mine, kissing her long and hard.

Sparks bounced between my heart and cock, two very different organs connected by this glorious woman.

I didn't think I'd ever love a woman like I loved Jasmin, but I hardly cared that Jasmin slept with Joe anymore. The anger that ravaged me months ago now felt like a strange memory.

Eva's lips moved across my jaw and down my neck, kissing and licking as she went, her hands working my buttons as she skidded her teeth over my collarbone.

"I don't care about the revenge anymore," I panted between kisses. "I just love being with you, Eva. I love —" Her lips crashed into mine, silencing my words. If *I love you* scared her, I'd wait. I'd wait forever for her.

It was freeing to just be with Eva, no pretenses, no games.

Her right hand slid into mine, and she brought it up her inner thigh, placing it securely between her legs.

"I'm so wet for you." She moved her panties aside and guided my fingers to her warm pussy, pressing them inside her. She groaned, and my cock became a steel beam of need.

I needed to feel her. I needed to enter her. I needed to satisfy her desires.

"If you entered me right now, I'd come instantly," she moaned.

"Fuck, Eva."

I was tempted to finger-fuck her to the point where my cock couldn't handle it and I blew my load in my pants.

My thumb swiped her clit, and she trembled against me. "This isn't over," she said, and it was almost a plea, like she was making sure this wasn't the last time.

"I never want it to be over," I said.

Her body tensed, and I swung my gaze to her face. Her eyes looked into mine with a moment of hesitation. She studied me, and I swear regret flashed behind her hazel eyes, but then it was gone and she was back to grinding my fingers with her hips.

"Fuck me, Ethan. I want your cock to ravish my pussy."

She made quick work of my zipper and buttons and shoved my pants down. Then she pressed me into my leather office chair and straddled me, her hips raised above my lap.

"You still clean?" she asked as she spread her knees wider, her feminine lips rubbing the tip of my cock.

The question startled me. How could she think I'd have been with anyone else since the hospital? Didn't she get it? I was hers. Completely.

But I didn't say it.

There was something that held me back. An inner knowing that she wasn't where I was yet. But she had to be close to loving me. She was here because she wanted to be with me.

This wasn't about getting back at Joe anymore. This was us coming together because I wanted her and she wanted me.

God, I was losing it. I was thinking about hearts and souls while her pussy was cresting my cock.

"I'm clean, baby. This cock is only yours."

She burrowed her face into my neck. It almost felt like she was hiding. Fuck, I needed to shut up. Eva wasn't ready for big declarations. Of course she wasn't.

She was still in a world of pain and confusion. But I'd be here for her when she was ready to hear how goddamn in love with her I was.

I dug my fingers into her hips and pressed her down, her slick lips sliding over my cock easily.

"Oh fuck, baby," I cried, burying my dick in her. "You feel so good."

Her hips shifted, sliding up my shaft, the little muscles gripping me like a Venus flytrap.

"Oh God." I shuddered, so close.

I licked my fingers and pressed them against her clit, rubbing her as she rode me.

Her head tilted backward, and I kissed the silky-smooth skin of her neck, licking her pulsing vein, sniffing her animal scent.

"Oh God, Ethan. Harder. Fuck me harder."

I did everything she asked. I slammed my cock into her and stroked her swollen mound. Her eyes squeezed shut and her head tilted back as her fingers dug into my shoulders so tight I knew there'd be marks tomorrow.

"Yes, baby," I cried, my orgasm swirling through my balls. "I'm gonna come so hard."

I clenched my jaw and held back my orgasm, waiting for her.

"Now, Ethan." She pressed her face into my neck, muffling her cries. "I'm coming. I'm coming."

Her pussy clenched my cock, her body shaking as

she came, and I exploded into her, pressing my mouth shut, swearing under my breath.

We rocked our bodies, lost in our ecstasy, releasing together. I clutched her to me, her body warm and supple. And I clung to her as if she were a lifeline. My orgasm heightened everything I was feeling, including my love for her.

"Damn, baby," I said into her hair. "I could do that every day for the rest of my life."

Eva rocked her head back and rested her forehead against mine, her sweet breath hot on my nose.

"Good," she said, her voice full of relief. "Come to the apartment tomorrow night. Before seven. And let's do it again."

I wrapped her in my arms and hugged her. "I'll be there."

As soon as I said it, she pressed herself off the chair, shoved her dress down, adjusted her panties back in place, and kissed me on the forehead.

"Great," she said. "See you tomorrow."

And then she was gone.

# Chapter 28

## *Eva*

I was almost giddy. After three months, I was taking my life back today even if I had to claw it out of Joe's and Ashley's hands.

Fuck Joe and his demands.

My revenge board was balanced against the couch. I ran my hand over the magazine cutouts and the written notes taped to it. There had been three phases to my revenge plan, and I was about to mark off the last one.

Phase one: Plot and implement revenge attacks to wreak havoc on Joe's life.

*Check.*

Phase two: "Catch" Joe and Ashley together and confront them.

*Check.*

Originally, phase two was meant to happen after my citizenship was secured, but I didn't need Joe for that anymore. If everything went as planned, there was another way I could stay in the country.

*Phase three*: Destroy Joe the same way he destroyed me.

The past three months felt like a strange nightmare with sporadic blips of euphoria, and to my astonishment, it was Ethan who had been the bright light in all the darkness.

My belly was raw from the emotional battle it had endured since the wedding, and it was time to pay it forward.

I looked in the mirror, inspecting my outfit, a red minidress with a bubble skirt. My lips were crimson to match.

Perfect.

I glanced at the clock. Ethan should be here any minute. A memory of yesterday in Ethan's office fluttered in my mind, and a sliver of guilt pressed against my ribs.

I'd tried to predict everything outcome of our endeavor. It hadn't been out of the realm of possibility that Ethan or I might catch feelings. But I'd put the percentage at less than ten.

But the last few times we'd been together he said things that stabbed me in my heart. I swear he almost said he loved me yesterday.

No. I shook my head. I couldn't think about that. Ignore. Push away. Do not be distracted. Keep your eye on the prize.

Joe needed to be eviscerated.

My belly was a swarm of buzzing bees. If this all went to shit, I'd be stung a thousand times, but if it went as I planned, there'd be lots of honey to feast on.

The intercom buzzed, and my nerves jumped. I pressed the button and unlocked the front door, getting into position.

It was happening. Phase three had commenced.

When I'd overheard Rachel and Ashley in the bathroom, the fury of a thousand scorned women had burned hot in my blood. All the plotting and scheming was not for nothing.

It was for this.

Ethan knocked on the open door and walked in. His face went from surprise to delight when he saw me in my red dress with my leg hiked up on the couch.

"Do you know why you've been called in for questioning?" I asked, hoping he'd play along.

"Fuck off," he said, and I resisted a smile. He understood and stepped right into the role. "I haven't done anything wrong."

I glanced between his legs.

"You're smuggling a very dangerous weapon," I said, my voice stern.

He laughed. Yeah, it was cheesy, but I was too anxious to be clever.

"This is serious," I said, dropping my voice. "Come here. Now."

He obeyed and stepped up to me, crowding me between the coffee table and sofa. His hand slid up my thigh, under my skirt, and his thumb brushed over my hip bone.

My gaze snagged on his mouth, and I bit back a sigh.

Ethan tilted his head until his lips were a breath away and tugged my hips against him, his hard-on pressing into my thigh.

I tipped my face forward and shortened the gap between us. The tip of his tongue poked out and glided along my upper lip. My knees wobbled, and he circled his left hand around my lower back and held me steady.

"I got you, baby," he whispered against my mouth, and a hot thrill rushed over my skin.

"Oh, Ethan," I breathed, a touch of sadness circling my insides. Would this be the last time I touched him?

I glanced at the clock on the wall, and the thought bolted away.

I sank to the cushions and dragged him on top of me, spreading my knees as his hips lowered and the soft fabric of his pants tickled my underwear.

My head tilted back, the curve of his lips locking with mine. His silky tongue slid into my mouth, grazing mine, and a wave of happiness came with it.

*God, I never want to leave this man.*

The thought came unbidden, and I tensed, forgetting the game for a moment.

Ethan spread his body flat against mine, heavy like a weighted blanket, safe and secure.

There was a sound outside the door, and I wrapped

my legs around Ethan's back and ground into his pelvis, my heart slamming against my ribs, anticipating the impending hurricane that was about to sweep us up.

The door rattled, metal on metal.

"Oh, Ethan. Yes, baby!" I moaned loudly as the door swung open.

"What the fuck!" Joe's booming voice erupted from the entryway where he stood gaping, Ashley behind him, her eyes wide but not nearly as shocked as Joe appeared.

Ethan shot his head around.

"Oh shit." Ethan hitched his hips back and scrambled off me, adjusting his pants. I shimmied my dress down and sat up.

We looked a mess. My hair was tangled and wild, my lips raw from being kissed. Ethan's mouth and face were smeared with my red lipstick, and his dark hair stuck up everywhere.

It was perfect.

"Motherfucker!" Joe leaped at Ethan, which is what I'd expected. Joe is so predictable.

I kicked my foot out, hitting Joe square in the groin before he touched Ethan.

"Ahhh." Joe crumpled, his hands holding his crotch. "My nuts!"

"I hope I obliterated them," I snarled, running my hands through my hair. "You deserve it, you narcissistic asshole."

Ashley leaned over Joe to help him, but he batted her off.

"I don't need any help."

I snatched my phone and got it ready.

"What the hell, man?" Joe asked, his breathing labored. "Did she drug you or something? You can't stand her."

But Ethan wasn't looking at Joe. He was staring at me, the little muscles in his jaw tense.

"Did you know they were gonna be here?" he asked.

I didn't answer and kept my gaze locked on Joe. It was a risk not telling Ethan, but I knew it would be more impactful if he was as shocked by the encounter as Joe and Ashley.

"You're not the only one who can keep a secret, Joe," I smirked. "I've been fucking Ethan for months."

Ethan's eyes widened, and he whipped his head to Joe and then back at me.

"You're lying," Joe said despite the evidence to the contrary.

"Who cares, babe," Ashley said, her hand petting Joe's forearm. "They mean nothing. Eva's gonna be gone soon and we can be together without hiding anything."

He shook off her hand, and Ashley stumbled sideways.

"You're getting nothing, you little bitch," Joe said to me, red splotches rushing up his neck and jaw. "I'm gonna sue you for everything." Then he shot his gaze at

Ethan. "And I'll make sure everyone knows how the altruistic Ethan Steele was fucking his best friend's wife. I'll ruin you."

"Not so fast," I said, clicking on our large flat-screen with the remote.

I turned on mirroring from my phone and hit play. Joe and Ashley filled the screen.

"What the..." Ashley stepped forward, her face turning a sickly shade of white.

A shot of Ashley flashed on the screen, her legs spread, her stomach squished in rolls, her face contorted. Joe's white ass shifted in front of the camera as he banged her from behind, his hairy balls filling the screen.

It was a video compilation of all the times they'd fucked in this room.

"If you do anything, I'll use this. I'll send it to your boss, Joe. He's a traditional family man, right? And I'll send it to Tiffany and Luis. I'll post it on both of your social media pages. I'll print screenshots and plaster them all over your neighborhoods."

Shortly after the wedding fiasco, I'd installed three nanny cams, one in the living room and one in each bedroom. The app was connected to my phone, and I'd been compiling the videos for months. Waiting.

"No!" Ashley snatched my phone and threw it on the floor. Then she took a metal candleholder from the coffee table and smashed it. The TV screen went blank.

"Hey!" I yelled, looking at my demolished phone.

I picked up the pieces, then shrugged. "Bashing my phone destroyed my phone. Not the evidence. Everything's stored in the cloud. I can access it whenever I want."

I crossed my arms over my chest; the satisfaction filled my bloodstream like a drug.

"You won't do it," Joe said, challenging me. "You're too weak."

I snapped my laptop open and maneuvered my finger over the mouse pad to the saved files. "Want to see more?"

"No!" Ashley moved toward Joe, her eyes wild. "Joe, do whatever she wants. I can't have that video out. And Ethan will ruin my career. He told me. He showed me."

I spun to Ethan, who was looking at me like he'd never seen me before. It was unnerving.

"What is she talking about?" I asked.

"Ashley saw us," he said, his voice strangely void of emotion. "At the hospital. That's why I ran out. I told her I'd wreck her career with scathing reviews that I'd post on all her business sites."

"At the top of the sites, Joe," Ashley said, her voice wobbling. "And he can do it. He's smart like that."

"He's not that fucking smart," Joe sneered. "He's an idiot for trusting Eva. I can't believe she opened her legs for you. She's the worst lay I've ever had."

"Because you suck at it, you selfish prick," I shot back. "Your baby dick couldn't get the job done."

"His dick isn't that small," Ashley shot back.

A shocked silence filled the room.

The saying goes, you could hear a pin drop. Right then, you could hear a strand of hair drop.

Joe's face was almost purple when he spoke next and he looked like he wanted to murder Ashley.

"Good luck, E." Joe laughed darkly, but his voice was shaky. "Her pussy dries up fast."

Ethan's hand shot out and hit Joe in the jaw. He flew backward and rolled over the coffee table. Ashley screamed. My hands flew to my mouth, shocked and a little delighted.

"Watch your mouth," Ethan growled.

Joe leaped to his feet but stumbled, unsteady after being punched. He cupped his jaw and glared at Ethan.

"I'm gonna fuck you up," he said, fire in his eyes.

"Like when you fucked Jasmin," I said.

Joe froze.

"I didn't—how did you—" Joe stammered.

"You slept with Jasmin?" Ashley asked. "Ethan's ex? Why would you..." Her voice trailed off, and she shook her head like she was trying to reorganize pieces of a puzzle.

"You're not so clever, Joe," I snapped. "And I'll make sure your baby dick is plastered everywhere if you try anything. Now get the fuck out of my apartment."

Ashley hesitated as Joe's gaze bounced between Ethan and me.

"You're gonna be sorry," Joe said, but the steam had gone out of his words.

"I'm already sorry," I said.

I took a step toward them, and Joe flinched.

"Get out."

They shuffled to the door, and Joe turned and said cooly, "This isn't over."

I stared at the closed door, my heart pounding.

"Wow," I said, a smile slowly spread across my face. "All those months of planning and we did it."

Across the room, Ethan stood very still. "Today was a setup."

"Yes," I said softly.

"You told Joe about Jasmin." Ethan's eyes narrowed. "That was my business."

I blinked rapidly. "Why are you mad?"

"Because you used me!" Ethan bellowed. "That's what yesterday was about, right? You were getting me ready for this moment. Making sure I would play my part."

He swiped his hand down his face, and when he looked at me, his gaze was dark.

"I told you yesterday I didn't care about the revenge anymore. You had every opportunity to tell me what tonight was about. But you didn't. You only cared about getting back at Joe," he grumbled.

"You did too!" I yelled. "It's why we started this."

"Things changed. You acted like you cared. I thought you—" His voice caught. "Forget it. You're right. This was about revenge. I'm an idiot."

Ethan stepped next to me, so close I felt the heat radiating from his skin. He leaned into me, but he didn't touch me.

"Did you know I loved you?" he whispered roughly in my ear.

I bit my lip and trembled.

"Yes." I breathed the word out.

"But you did it anyway." Ethan walked to the door and yanked it open. "Payback was all you cared about."

"Wait!"

A dart of panic scraped down my esophagus, landing in my gut.

"Congratulations, Eva. You did it. You won."

"Ethan, please," I begged, my throat burning. "I'm sorry I didn't tell you. I was scared you'd say no. I saw the look in your eyes yesterday, and I was afraid you were going to break our promise, so I didn't tell you." A whimper caught in my throat. "I didn't know...I didn't realize."

"You knew exactly what you were doing." Ethan slammed his fist onto the entry table, and I jumped.

"The only thing I needed from you was trust," he said. "And you just obliterated it."

I reached for him, but he stepped through the doorway and into the hallway.

"Ethan—"

"Don't," he rasped.

I opened my mouth to protest, to tell him I was a fool and I'd felt those big, scary feelings too, but the look of repulsion in his eyes shattered any vestiges of hope in my heart.

"I can't do this again." Ethan cleared the door, and it slammed in my face.

The bittersweet dregs of revenge circled my gut and soured in my mouth. I thought Joe's affair was the worst thing that could happen to me.

I was wrong.

# Chapter 29

## *Ethan*

There was a rustling in the hallway. I rolled over and threw the pillow over my head and tried to disappear into the mattress and back into the relief of sleep.

The doorknob rattled, and someone walked in. By the sound of the footfalls and the fact that only my sister was home—except for Beau, who couldn't crawl yet—it had to be Savi invading my tomb.

"Get up, bum." She pressed the pillow covering my head hard.

"No," I mumbled into the mattress.

"You stink. It's offending my nose, and Brynn's gonna be home from daycare soon. Come on. You've only showered once since you got here, and I'm not sure you even used soap."

I groaned and slid out of bed, my stench following me into the bathroom in the hallway. I scooped out the kid toys and baby bathtub and turned on the water. When it was steaming, I stepped inside, yanked the curtain closed, and let the water pour down my back.

It had been almost two weeks since the confrontation with Joe. He hadn't called once. During the first few days, Eva called and texted all day, every day. Eventually, I blocked her number.

If I ignored her long enough, she'd go away.

I'd tried to focus on the foundation, but my mind was locked on Eva, and at the end of last week, I told my team I was taking time off and then crawled into bed and slept for two days until my sister arrived with the kids in tow and dragged me to her house.

I dried off and put on fresh clothes, but the guest bed had been stripped. I turned in a circle, then snatched the comforter from the ground and climbed back on the bed and threw it over me.

Savi yanked it off.

"You're not going to bed," Savi said, Beau straddling her hip, sucking on a small giraffe toy. "Come outside and get something besides despair in your lungs."

Begrudgingly, I followed her into her small backyard.

"Why did she do it?" I said, plonking into a nylon hammock strung between two trees. The warm breeze felt nice but didn't soothe the massive hole in the middle of my chest.

"Ask her," Savi said.

She laid a blanket on the ground and put Beau

down on his tummy. He gurgled and giggled, and I leaned over and rubbed his downy-soft head.

"Hey, buddy," I said, my heart fluttering a teeny tiny bit.

"I already know the answer." I laid my head back and looked up at the leaves swaying above my head, beams of sunlight hitting my face. "This weather sucks."

"It's gorgeous outside." Savi laughed. "It's always gorgeous here."

My inner thoughts were a record stuck on repeat, and I was getting sick of it, but I couldn't stop them.

When she'd left my office the day before the blowup, I'd floated home. I'd been high on my realization that I loved her, and I'd believed things had changed for her too, that she was on her way to loving me.

But we'd been in two universes. Her universe was getting back at Joe. My universe was her.

"It's my own fault," I grumbled, fisting the sides of the hammock. "I pretended what we were doing was real."

"It wasn't?" Savi asked.

"I really liked her, and I thought she…" I trailed off, embarrassed to say it aloud.

"You thought she felt the same way," Savi said gently. "You need to talk to Eva. Tell her that you're in lo—"

"Don't say it," I warned, my heart seizing.

"You're not mad at Eva for using you. You're mad

because you think she doesn't love you. But you don't know anything, Ethan. She texted you all those apologies. She begged you to see her. If she was only using you, she wouldn't care that she hurt you."

I swung a sidelong gaze at her. "Have you been reading my texts?"

"Yes."

"Ugh." I slammed my fist into my thigh. "Don't read my texts, Savi."

Beau whimpered at my outburst, and I reached down, scooped him up, and placed him on my chest, rubbing his back and rocking the hammock gently back and forth. He dropped his head to my bicep and stuck his thumb in his mouth.

The ice around my heart melted.

"Don't defend her. She was on the warpath, and I was the ammunition."

"Why are you hiding away here? You don't run from problems, you fix them," Savi said.

I rested my hand on Beau and it eclipsed his little back. He breathed calmly under my palm, and my heart rate tapered.

"I love this guy," I said.

"I know."

"And I'm not hiding, but I can't be in my apartment. I spent a week there feeling sorry for myself, and all I saw was her. I swear I could smell her in the walls. And she'd only been there a few times. Anywhere in the city would've been too close to her." I rubbed my hand gently on Beau's head, and his eyes fluttered closed.

Savi had always stepped in when I was younger. She'd come home from college and see that I was stressed, hiding in my room, and she'd scream at our parents for being weak assholes who should never have had children.

That was the only time I saw my parents united. They vehemently defended their marriage. What else could they do? If they admitted they hated each other and that they'd stayed for all the wrong reasons, that would mean everything they'd done for the past two decades had been wrong.

My parents were so adamant we were wrong about them that they waited two years after I went to college to divorce. Mom said she stayed because Dad got sober, but he'd been clean for three years before I left high school.

Screw them.

Savi and I were fucked up in major ways because they chose to stay in a toxic relationship rather than divorce when we were kids.

Savi had buckets of therapy and forgave our parents and had a moderately good relationship with our mom. Dad came around once a year to play the doting grandfather with her children, but like his relationship with me, he was mainly absent unless he wanted something.

"Who's coming over?" I asked, closing my eyes. "Mom?"

"No one. What are you talking about?"

"You made me shower. You made me get out of my room. And you keep checking your phone."

She sighed loudly. "Fine. Someone's coming over, but it's not Mom. Just keep an open mind."

I shot up. At the last second I remembered Beau and clutched him to my chest so he didn't fall. The sudden movement woke him, and he wailed. I bounced him, trying to soothe him, but he screamed bloody murder.

"Please tell me he's not yours," a woman said from across the backyard.

Every muscle in my body tensed at the familiar voice, and prickles rushed over my skin.

Jasmin.

# Chapter 30

## *Ethan*

"Hey, E," Jasmin said, walking across the grassy lawn.

She wore a colorful patterned skirt and a bright orange top with large dragonfly earrings. It was a typical Jasmin outfit, bright and cheery.

When she walked into a room, her glow always seeped into me, lighting me up. Today, she was radiant, but I felt none of the luminance I once did.

It had been almost two years since I'd last seen her. We broke up right before the summer of our senior year, and she went home to her parents in Atlanta for the break. By the fall semester, she'd transferred to UGA for her final year. When I found out, I'd been relieved, hoping I'd never see her again.

I never thought I'd find her standing in my sister's backyard while I held a crying baby.

Jasmin half smiled, her full lips painted a bright pink that popped against her umber skin.

"Your hair's...gone," I said, too stunned to utter anything except what I saw before me. When we'd been together, she'd switch between long braids and her natural tight curls.

Savi rolled her eyes and carefully took Beau from my arms. His crying stopped as soon as she held him.

Jasmin ran her hand over her shaved head.

"It looks great," I said.

She looked really good. And transformed. It wasn't the hair, though. There was something else about her I couldn't articulate.

"I went a little mad after we broke up." She laughed self-consciously. "That's when I first shaved my head. But I loved it. It was like I came out of a cocoon and transformed into who I was meant to be, and I never went back."

"Why did you call her?" I asked Savi as she tried to sidle inside through the back door.

"I'm glad she called," Jasmin said and took a step closer.

Savi closed the door without an explanation, and I was alone with Jasmin. A woman I thought I'd never get over. A woman who'd cluttered my brain and made me want to punch everything in sight when she broke up with me.

I crossed my arms and huffed out a short breath through my nose. "You can leave. I said all I wanted to say the day you dumped me."

Jasmin tucked her chin back, startled.

"*You* dumped *me*."

I stumbled over one of Beau's toys, her words literally knocking me off-balance. Was she delusional?

"It was the morning after we'd brought that couple back to my place from that bar, the one with the mechanical bull." She put her left hand on her hip and pointed her right finger accusingly at me. "But when we started to hook up with them, you got all mad and kicked them out. The next day you said you couldn't be with other people while you were in a relationship. I told you I wasn't ready for a big commitment. I wanted to experiment and have fun with other people. I wanted us to do it together, but you said no. You said if I wanted to be with anyone else, we couldn't be together. I didn't want to break up, but you said you couldn't be that person."

I turned away from Jasmin and the memory she'd laid at my feet. My head ached, and I dropped my forehead in my hands, massaging my temple. All I recalled was walking out of her apartment and into Joe's and fuming in the shower (while kicking every shampoo, conditioner, body wash, and crotch wash bottle at my feet).

"No," I said, shaking my head violently. "No. You broke up with me."

"Fuck, Ethan. I loved you. I was devastated. Our relationship felt like a cage, and when I tried to break free that night and take you with me, you screamed at me and told me you were done if that's what I wanted."

She stepped up behind me, and her rose-scented perfume enveloped me. The smell transported me back to those days, and I ground my jaw, forcing the nostalgia away.

"I was so mad that morning," I said, speaking as it came back to me. "I thought you were wrecking our relationship."

"It was already wrecked," Jasmin said gently. Her hand touched my shoulder, and I flinched, spinning on her.

She put her hands up and took a step back.

"You have a lot more anger in you than you did when we dated." She smiled ruefully. "That's good. I always thought you needed to fight for what you wanted. And you did. Look what you made of yourself. You used to talk about that app idea but you were too caught up in me and what you thought we were to do anything about it."

After we broke up and after I'd raged and after I'd sulked, all this space opened up for me to create. That's when I worked in earnest on the app that would become Potty Please.

"You thought our relationship was perfect, but it never was. You like predictability and order, I like spontaneity. When you said it was over, I was crushed, but I wasn't going to make you change to fit into a mold that wasn't you."

The world was going topsy-turvy, and I was off-kilter. Everything I thought I knew was in disarray, and I couldn't put it back together in a way that made sense.

"You couldn't have been that heartbroken. You

slept with Joe," I spat, dropping the bomb at her feet. I watched her carefully, wondering if she'd lie.

Jasmin's face paled, and the tiny freckles on her nose popped out. "He told you?"

"I saw the emails."

"I was really pissed at you," she said, avoiding my gaze. "And it was stupid and immature and a horrible thing to do, but yeah. I did it. He saw me in a bar one night. I'd been drinking, and he took me home. Nothing happened that night. But the next day he emailed me and—"

"I don't need a play-by-play."

"Right. Sorry." Jasmin placed her hand on my arm, squeezing gently. "I really am sorry. I'd never been hurt like that, and I was running wild, sleeping with a lot of people and figuring out who I was. I'm sorry I hurt you, but I don't believe in regret. I did my best in the moment, and it wasn't pretty, but I'm happy now. And I hope you can be happy too. Life's messy, Ethan. The sooner you learn to get dirty, the sooner you'll find your joy."

"Did you see that on a TikTok?" I asked wryly.

"Oprah."

I smiled.

There was an ease about her that she didn't have when we were together. That's what was different. It was the confidence of someone who knew who they were and wasn't afraid.

The tension in my shoulders loosened, and I closed my eyes in a long blink.

"I'm glad you came," I said.

She huffed out a snort-laugh. "I'm not sure I believe you. But thank you." She opened her arms. "Can I hug you?"

I grabbed her and pulled her into a tight hug, almost violent, but she squeezed me back, meeting my fervor. She could always give as hard as she got.

It was a hug full of sorries and regrets and forgiveness.

"I have to go," Jasmin said and stepped back, wiping her eyes. "But listen. It's a wonderful thing when you let your crazy out because you realize you're not crazy at all. You're just you. Beautiful, imperfect you."

She walked to the fence but stopped at the open gate. "And when you find someone who loves your crazy, don't fucking let go."

# Chapter 31

## *Eva*

A chill swept through the office, and I shivered. Someone had left a window cracked. I rolled my chair to the bank of windows and tugged down the offender.

It had been one long month since my confrontation with Joe and Ashley. One month since I ruined my relationship with Ethan. One month since all happiness evaporated into sad wisps of regret.

My life consisted of two parts now. Before and after.

A bubble of sadness pressed painfully against my throat like it always did when I thought about the day I ruined everything.

"Dammit," I muttered.

"What's wrong?" The new hire, Cody, glanced up from his workstation. He was younger than me, a hard worker, and kept mostly to himself, but I liked him. He was eager and bright.

"Nothing," I said, forcing a smile. "Just inane work stuff."

Alexis walked into the office and Cody's eyes lit up but he spun back to his computer and typed rapidly, his cheeks turning rosy.

My throat tightened, and I resisted warning him against an office crush. That crush could turn into something more. And that something more could destroy his happiness.

Okay, maybe I wasn't okay.

I missed Ethan.

There it was. The gut-wrenching, can't-sleep, hate-my-life truth.

But what could I do?

I'd tried to contact him, but after weeks of unanswered calls and texts, the message was clear. Ethan had blocked me from his life.

Ethan had said he loved me and then took it back. No do-overs. No repeats. No forgiveness.

"Hart!" Derrick hollered from his office doorway across the office.

I jumped a foot off my chair at his booming voice and scurried to gather my iPad and phone.

"Coming!"

At his door, I stopped dead in my tracks. Rachel stood next to Derrick's desk. Alexis was there too, sitting in Derrick's chair.

"What's going on?" I asked, suspicious.

Derrick shut the door and ushered me to one of the armchairs across from the desk.

"Sit," he instructed.

"Is this an intervention?" I asked, trying for a joke, but my heart was racing.

"Yes," Rachel said.

"Oh." I turned to Alexis. "Why are you here? Are you going to therapy me?"

She laughed. "No. Prathi's out of town, so I'm stepping in as the HR rep." She smiled kindly and tucked a strand of her auburn hair behind her ear.

"The thing is," Rachel began, "you're getting on everyone's nerves."

"Hey!" I protested.

"You keep whining about Ethan, but you won't do anything about it." Rachel raised a pierced eyebrow. "And it's affecting your work. You might get fired."

I swung my gaze at Derrick.

"Is that true?"

"No," he said and narrowed his gaze in warning at Rachel. "Don't be an asshole."

"She's my best friend. It's my job."

"I'm doing my best." I crossed my arms. "I'm allowed to mope. My heart's broken. It's part of the healing journey. Drink too much. Cry at sappy love songs. Annoy your friends by overanalyzing everything and asking what you should have done instead. Torturing yourself by going on their social media pages. It's in the broken heart rule book."

"There's no such thing," Derrick said.

"There should be." Alexis snorted, then clamped her mouth shut. "Sorry. I'm just an observer."

"What do you want me to do? Put on a fake smile and act like I'm happy when I'm devastated?"

"No, you idiot." Rachel flicked a paperclip at me. "I want you to tell Ethan how you feel."

"He knows," I said.

"You said the words *I love you*?" Rachel asked, already knowing the answer.

"Um, no. But I apologized. I sent him a stupid shirt with flamingos all over it. I went to his apartment and rang his intercom for an hour. And then I went back and did it again. I sent him SVU memes for God's sake."

"But you never said the words!" Rachel threw her hands up.

"I didn't know I loved him until he was gone!" I yelled and then slumped in the chair.

"The poor guy was in love with you, and he thinks you used him. Which you did." Rachel clucked. "But you also fell in love with him, and he doesn't know that. You have to tell him."

I pushed the chair back and stood. "Nope."

Derrick stepped in front of me, blocking my exit.

"Why are you in on this?" I asked.

"Rachel brought me in because she needs my resources," he said.

"What's he talking about?" I frowned, annoyed but curious.

"You're gonna do the big gesture," Rachel said.

"The what?"

"Like in the movies!" Alexis said, a wide grin on

her petite features. "Sorry. I'm just excited. I've never been part of something like this. Not that I'm part of it. I'm just an observer."

She sat back but the smile stayed.

"At the end of every stupid Hallmark movie, the character makes a fool of themselves and confesses their love."

I shook my head. "No way."

"Shhh," Rachel said. "You've been blathering on for over a month about Ethan. Now you're gonna do something."

Rachel turned the whiteboard next to her around. The title at the top read *Operation Ethan*. Under it was a list of action steps.

There were five items on the list. I read through them, and by the end my heart was thumping and my face was hot.

"Derrick, you're okay with this?" I asked.

"Yeah. I've already talked to my guys. They're in. You just say when."

I scratched my neck.

"This could go really bad," I said, my entire midsection churning.

"Ethan will love it," Rachel said.

"Or he'll reject me and I'll be humiliated."

"Then you'll basically be back where you are right now but at least you'll finally know."

"I already know," I said.

"No, you don't," Derrick said.

I blinked. He sounded so sure.

"You're afraid," he said.

I looked at the three sets of eyes and then exhaled, staring at the floor.

All the times Ethan and I had been together rushed through my mind. He'd been there for me from the moment this all began. He went along with every ridiculous revenge idea, including the affair.

At the hospital, when Ethan held me, I'd felt it then. The flutters of love. But I couldn't acknowledge that something real was happening. I wasn't ready.

"I can't be rejected again," I said, gripping my stomach. "Two heartbreaks in one year are too much."

"Ethan loves you," Rachel said.

"How do you know?" I asked.

"If he was over you, he wouldn't be working this hard to avoid you."

The truth of that trickled in and my resolve faltered.

"She's gonna do it." Rachel beamed.

"Wait. I didn't say—"

"Come on. I want my friend back," Rachel whined. "This may be the best thing you ever do. And we're all here for you no matter what happens."

I looked around the room, and I knew each of them would support me no matter what happened.

It was Derrick who saved my ass and made it possible for me to finally confront Joe. Derrick had offered to have the company sponsor my work visa. That's what he told me that day in his office when I'd seen the notification from the nanny cam that Joe and Ashley were at the apartment.

I didn't know Alexis that well, but she'd been there the first day we cooked up the revenge idea, and she seemed as excited for me as Rachel.

I snatched the whiteboard and slid my arm over the surface, erasing the list.

Rachel's shoulders sank.

"I'm tired of being predictable," I said, breaking the board in two.

"Uh, that's company property," Derrick said.

Rachel threw an eraser at him. He ducked and it crashed into the window.

"Never mind," Derrick amended.

"Okay," I said, a smile creeping over my lips. "Let *Operation Ethan* commence."

# Chapter 32

## *Ethan*

Noise erupted outside my office door. It was late, after nine in the evening, and I was the only one left in the office. I'd buried myself in work since I got back in town last week.

After Jasmin left, I packed my small bag, kissed my niece and nephew, and went home. But it was lonely in the loft with my circling thoughts dragging me back to every encounter with Eva and all the what-ifs.

My conversation with Jasmin had been healing, and my rage over her deception with Joe had dissipated. For too long I'd let the fury churn inside me and fuel my wild behavior with Eva. But if I'd never found out about their betrayal, I never would've gone along with Eva's wild antics.

And that scared me.

These past few months had been more fun than I'd had in my whole life. How had I not seen what an amazing, funny, bright woman Eva was from the start?

Yeah, she'd gone a little psycho, but who wouldn't after what Joe put her through?

I liked her kind of crazy.

I admired her for taking action and grabbing her life back and saying fuck you to Joe and Ashley.

Somehow it made me love her more.

Jasmin's version of what happened with Joe hadn't been easy to hear, but it lessened the sting. It didn't feel like such a betrayal. At least from her side.

Joe, on the other hand, was still a dick.

The asshole never reached out after he caught Eva and me and discovered I knew all about Jasmin and him. I wasn't expecting an apology, and I'd purposely wrecked any chances at reconciliation once I'd slept with Eva. But I thought he'd at least show up at my door looking for a fight.

Joe didn't contact me, but his mom did. Tiffany said Eva had called her and told her that Joe and she were getting a divorce. When Tiffany pressed Eva, Eva wouldn't rat on Joe.

After a failed attempt to get the story out of Joe, Tiffany called me. I had no problem filling Tiffany in on what really happened. Not the Eva-and-I-had-an-affair-and-then-we-blackmailed-Joe part. But the Joe-cheated-on-Eva part.

I received a text with a lot of *fuck yous* and *see you next Tuesdays* from Joe after that.

Right back at you, fucker.

Thundering footsteps outside my office door

vibrated my desk, and I pushed my rolling chair back. What the hell was going on?

I cracked the door to investigate, and three men dressed in business suits and holding badges charged in.

"What's going on?"

One of the larger men with shoulders almost as wide as my doorframe snatched my arm and spun me around, pressing my cheek into the top of my desk.

"What the fuck," I said, my heart rate zipping into a gallop.

"Ethan Steele?" the man asked.

"Yes."

"Do you know Evelyn Hart?"

My stomach twisted.

"Is she in trouble?" I tried to turn and look at the other men filing into the room but a sharp pain shot through my arm where it was pinned behind my back.

"We're with ICE." He flipped a badge in front of my face but took it back before I could read it. "We received a tip that you assisted her with an illegal marriage."

"It wasn't...it was a love marriage but—"

"Don't waste your breath on me. You can tell the court after we bring you in."

"What?" I strained against the behemoth behind me but he kicked the rolling chair toward me, bumping my knees so I fell into the chair, and he handcuffed each wrist to a chair arm.

"What is this?" I asked, suddenly suspicious. Law enforcement wouldn't handcuff me to a chair.

The brute spun the chair so I faced the back of my office. There was shuffling behind me, people going out and in, people whispering, then the door clicked shut.

"Hello?" I tried to twist my head around but someone held the back of my skull and forced my gaze forward.

"Keep still, dirtbag."

Every nerve in my body froze. "Eva?"

"I said shut up."

I blinked, trying to get a grip on what the fuck was happening.

"No, you didn't," I said. "You said *'Keep still, dirtbag.'*"

With a push from my left foot, I spun the chair around, and Eva lost her grip.

She stood before me in a slim-fit navy skirt suit and a brown, shoulder-length wig. There was a badge clipped onto her jacket pocket.

"What are you doing?" I asked, glancing behind her, my mind still whirling after the light roughing up I got from the ogre. "Who were those guys?"

Eva kicked my chair with her black heels, and it rolled into the desk. "I'll ask the questions."

"Can you take these off?" My wrists were still in the handcuffs attached to the chair's arms on either side of my thighs.

"Shut it," she said with more force. "You're not going anywhere until you answer my questions."

I narrowed my gaze but said nothing.

She tugged her jacket off, folded it neatly, and placed it on the desk next to me, stepping closer. The four walls of the room closed in on me and every nerve in my body was aware of Eva's presence.

"You're here because you're an asshole." She crossed her arms and raised an eyebrow.

"Excuse me?" I asked, shooting my gaze up to her hazel eyes.

"You're worse than Joe," she continued.

"Fuck you, Eva." I ground my jaw. How could she compare me to him?

"Fuck you, Ethan," she said without hesitation.

I dropped my chin and shook my head back and forth, laughing lightly.

"You think this is a joke?" she asked, a shake in her voice, giving away her nerves.

The glimpse of vulnerability was an arrow to my heart, and I stopped laughing and met her gaze full-on.

"Why the handcuffs?"

"You deserve them," she said, her gaze hardening.

"Why?"

She bent forward and touched my nose with her nose, her two eyes becoming one. Then she slid her cheek against my face and her lips landed on my ear and she whispered, "You told me you loved me."

Her wig tickled my neck as she rocked back and folded her arms, waiting for my response.

"I did love you."

Her face collapsed and she spun her back to me.

"But you don't anymore?" she asked softly.

I didn't answer. My fingers twitched, wanting to slide up her arms and turn her to me so I could see her face. But my wrists were trapped, and I was wary of why she was here.

"I didn't do anything wrong," she spoke softly, almost to herself. "I know I should've told you Joe and Ashley were coming that night, but I didn't want them to know it was staged and I was scared you would've said no. It sounds awful, and it probably was, but it was important to me at the time. If I'd known I'd lose you —" Her voice cracked. She paused and then said, "I'd never have done it."

My throat tightened hearing the pain in her voice.

"Turn around."

"No," she said, her voice thick with tears.

I rattled the handcuffs again. "Let me out of these," I growled.

"No," she huffed.

"Dammit, Eva! Turn around."

A tremble shook her from head to toe, but she finally turned around, and when she saw my face, her perfect lips popped open in surprise.

"Why are you crying?" she asked.

"Why do you think, crazy girl?"

She bit her bottom lip, her brow furrowed in confusion.

"You left me," she said. "I'm the one who should be upset."

"I didn't leave. I was angry and I needed time. You

can't blame me for that." I waited for her to meet my gaze. "I'm not your father."

"Thank God," she said through the wetness in her voice. "That would be awkward."

Her little joke gave me hope. I lifted my wrists, the metal clanging against metal. "Can you unlock these?"

"No," she said, sniffing her tears away. Her wig was crooked, and it was the cutest damn thing.

"Why not?" I asked, a hint of annoyance in my voice.

"Not until you tell me why you said you loved me."

"Why do I have to be restrained to have this talk?" I asked, my patience waning.

"I like to be in control," she said simply.

I barked a laugh. "I'm aware."

"Don't laugh at me," she said, wetness filling her eyes again.

"I'm not," I said calmly.

She sank to the floor, kneeling in front of me.

"It was cruel to tell me you loved me and then disappear from my life," she said, her voice low but gaining momentum as she continued. "It was like you ripped my heart out of my chest and stuck a knife through it. I can't think. I can't breathe. I can't do anything."

"Why?"

"Because I only want you." Her chin wobbled as she fought back the tears that glistened in her eyes, and she bashed the heels of her palms into her eyes, trying to stop the flow of tears.

"Eva, don't cry." I yanked and pulled at the cuffs. "Eva, please. Listen."

I needed her to hear me. To say all the things that had been tumbling around my brain for months.

"You didn't lose me," I yelled, standing and banging the chair wheels on the ground. Desperation eclipsed my sanity, and when her red-rimmed eyes met mine, I softened my voice. "You never lost me. I'm desperately in love with you. Okay? I love you, Eva."

Eva wrapped her arms around my calves, dragging me to her, and she buried her face in my lap, hugging my thighs. I tugged her wig off and dug my hands into her hair, cradling her head in my lap. I was still cuffed but I could reach this part of her.

Goddammit. If this woman didn't love me back, I'd never recover.

"You had me at dirtbag," I said through a soft laugh. "You had me at dirtbag."

# Chapter 33

## *Eva*

I kept my head buried in Ethan's lap, scared to meet his eyes. He loved me.

*Ethan Steele loved Eva Hart.*

I shuddered, and Ethan leaned over and kissed the back of my head tenderly.

From my back pocket, I pulled out the key and undid his handcuffs. He clamped his hands around my waist and dragged me into his lap.

My hair stuck to my face, sweaty from the wig, and he brushed it back, cupping my cheeks and tugging my face to him.

"Wait," I said, looking into his blue eyes. "I'm sorry I used you. You deserve so much more." My voice caught, and Ethan brushed his thumb back and forth over my jaw. "You were there for me at my ugliest, lifting me up and never shaming me. It's not all Joe's fault what happened."

"It doesn't excuse his cheating," Ethan quickly said, his voice rumbling in his chest.

"Of course not. But he was right. Once I said yes to his proposal, I was completely focused on the wedding. I treated the nuptials and our relationship like a job, and Joe was an employee I told where to go and what to do as I ticked off my tasks. It wasn't like that with you. We had a mission, but it was fun in a deranged way. There's a freedom when I'm with you, and it feels fucking amazing. I want to feel that way for the rest of my life. With you."

Ethan's left palm cupped the base of my neck and pulled me to him. This time, I let him.

"I need you to say it," he whispered against my mouth, his left hand gripping my right thigh. I shifted my knees, pressing them into the side of his thigh as I straddled his lap. "Fucking say it, because I'm about to wreck you."

My gaze swung back and forth between his eyes, taking in the unabashed love and volcanic desire in his gaze. An electric current filled with tenderness zipped down my throat and struck me in the middle of my chest.

"I love you," I said, unable to contain it. "I love you so fucking much."

"It's about damn time." His hands cupped my ass, and he lifted us out of the chair and swung me into the wall beside his desk, the frames next to my head rattling.

His mouth crashed into mine, and I opened my lips

just before contact. His tongue slid in, rubbing mine urgently.

"Fuck, I love you so much, baby." He devoured my mouth, his hands digging into my ass, my fingers tangling in his hair.

"I love you too, Ethan." My heart swelled so fast it felt like my ribs would break.

"You're wearing too many damn clothes," he grumbled, unbuttoning my blouse with swift fingers and yanking it from my arms.

He took both my hands into one of his and raised my arms above my head, pinning me to the wall. His other hand traced the bottom hem of my skirt, brushing my inner thigh. My stomach hollowed out under his touch.

"You're mine," he said possessively.

"And you're mine. Both of you." I bucked my hips forward, tapping his enlarged cock.

His grip on my thighs faltered.

"Jesus, Eva," he groaned, his features covered in need...desperate, glorious need. My sex clenched at his raw desire.

"If I stroked you right now, how fast would you come?" I asked. God, sex was fun.

"It would be too humiliating to admit," he said.

I tugged my hands free and dropped to my knees, my face at his crotch. "How many licks to the center of a Tootsie Pop?"

His cock twitched inside his pants, and I was done. My panties were drenched. I needed Depends.

"I'm warning you," he said, desperation in his voice.

My bottom lip popped out, aroused by his honesty.

"My pussy's Niagara because of you," I admitted.

Ethan laughed and then yanked me up from under my armpits and pinned me back against the wall.

"I want to feel your dam break."

He jammed his hand up my skirt and into my panties, sliding his finger between my folds.

"You weren't joking, baby." His eyes glazed and his thumb circled my clit in small, luxurious strokes.

"Oh God, Ethan." Thoughts were taken from me, and all that was left were his hands on my throbbing sex.

"You like that, baby?" He panted against my neck, fucking me with his fingers, rubbing my clit to the point of insanity.

"So much." My pussy clamped around his fingers. My hips jerked and my ass hit the wall and bounced forward, filling me until his fingers were buried to the hilt.

"I'm close," I gasped. The swirling waves of pleasure circled rapidly, lifting me up and tossing me around in a frantic wave. My fingers dug into his shoulders, his thumb circling and massaging and pressing down on my bud, which was slick from my juices leaking out. "Right there. Faster. Oh God. Yes!"

My pelvis spasmed, my head whipping back so fast it hit the wall behind me and stars circled me. I screamed, riding my orgasm. Ethan continued his plea-sure assault until I was a wet noodle in his arms.

"I'm Gumby," I said, panting into his hair.

"I'm not done." Ethan kissed me lightly on the lips. "You're gonna come again all over my dick until I'm dripping out of you."

Ethan flipped me over and yanked my skirt off, my panties flying across the room.

I liked Ethan like this, assertive and bullish.

He sprawled me over his desk facedown. Pens and loose papers dug into my ribs, but I barely felt them. I heard his zipper run down the track of his pants and I shifted, watching him from over my shoulder. He shoved his pants down, and when his cock sprang free, he groaned like an animal being uncaged.

Ethan choked the root of his cock and rubbed it over my bare ass as my pussy contracted.

"Your cock is so beautiful," I said, my sex tingling.

"Fuckity fuck, Eva," Ethan ground out, pre-cum dripping from his bulbous head. "Don't say that shit. I can barely contain this."

I was spent from my orgasm but fuck if I didn't want his thickness to fill me up and stretch me out.

He spread my cheeks wide, staring hungrily at my pussy.

"I want you as desperate for release as I am," he said and buried his face in my ass. He spread me almost to the point of pain and sucked my clit into his mouth.

"Holy shit," I yelled. He sucked it like it was a

straw and he needed to get to the lifesaving elixir at the bottom.

He was unrelenting, and dammit, I'd never experienced anything like it. The only thing close was a suctioning sex toy that I thought no man could ever emulate. But here Ethan was, sucking me to the point I was almost coming again.

"Stop!" I yelled, and he released me. "What"—I breathed out—"the hell was that?"

He shrugged, a smug look on his handsome face. "A trick I learned."

"From who?" I asked, darkness hovering over me as I thought of him doing this to some other woman.

I might have to kill all his exes.

"The internet."

I laughed, but then he spread my cheeks again and lifted his cock to my entrance, sliding his steel rod back and forth along my opening, and I clamped my mouth shut.

"Are you close?" he asked, his voice shaky. "'Cause once I enter you, it's over. My balls won't be able to contain this eruption."

"My pussy's gonna be the size of the Goodyear Blimp if you don't shut up and enter me right fucking now," I warned.

His tip spread my lips, entering me inch by excruciating inch. His breathing was labored, like he was carrying a bag of cement up a hill.

I couldn't take it. I hitched my hips up and slammed back, his cock filling me to the brink.

He cried out like he'd been mauled by a wild animal. Which he had.

"Don't," he gritted through his teeth. "Don't fucking move."

"Touch me," I said.

With great care he leaned forward and fingered my clit, spreading the wetness that seeped out of my lips over it.

"I'm close, baby," I said, my orgasm swirling into my hips, readying to take flight.

I tightened my grip around his cock.

"Oh God," Ethan said, his fingers digging into my hip as he pumped back and forth, my ass cheeks slamming into his pelvis, the electric currents swirling around my clit and through the little muscles in my sex as if they were one glorious symbiotic organism.

"I'm coming!" I shouted as it overtook me. "Again. I'm coming again!"

I could hardly believe it.

"Oh shit!" Ethan cried out, shuddering. His release sent me over the edge, our slick bodies sliding together.

When we were both floppy shells of human beings, we slid to the floor, wrapped in each other's limbs.

I inched closer, snuggling in tight, but I couldn't get close enough. I wanted to crawl inside him like Luke Skywalker and the creature in *Return of the Jedi*. Gross. But that's what I wanted.

"You feel like home," I said, then burrowed my head in Ethan's chest. "Damn, that was cheesy."

Ethan's arms clamped me so tight it was hard to

breathe, but I'd never felt safer.

"We're swimming in cheese, and I fucking love it."

I laughed into the hard muscle of his pec. "Why?"

"Because it means we're in love."

I wiggled until I faced him and sighed when I met his eyes.

There was banging on the closed office door, and I yelped, covering my naked bits.

"Hey, Ms. Hart. You done with us?" came a deep voice from the other side. It was one of Derrick's cop buddies that helped me out today. "Oh shit. Sorry, Vince. I thought you guys had gone."

"Nah. I wanted to make sure that guy didn't rough you up."

I bit back a laugh. "Nope. Um, you guys can go. And thank you!"

Booted footsteps faded, and I settled back into Ethan's arms.

"Those were Derrick's friends," I explained. "Rachel thought I should do a big romantic gesture."

Ethan intertwined his fingers with mine.

"That was your idea of romance?" Ethan asked, kissing my knuckles.

"Too kinky?" I asked, a light blush heating my cheeks. Ethan made me bold, and I fucking loved it.

"You're a bad girl." He kissed me. "In the best way."

The kiss deepened, and I flipped him on his back and stretched his arms above his head like he had done to me earlier against the wall. Between my legs, his cock grew hard, and I lowered against him with a moan.

My gaze caught on the discarded handcuffs next to Ethan's head.

"Oh crap. I forgot to give back the cuffs." I strained to reach them, but Ethan snagged them first.

"Let's keep them." Ethan's light eyes twinkled with a naughty glint. "I'm sure we can find some creative uses for them."

I lowered my head until our mouths touched. My toes curled, and heat shot into my heart, warming me to my soul.

"I'll make a list!" I trilled and sank into his arms.

"Are you ready for that kind of commitment?" Ethan joked, but there was wariness in his voice.

"Actually," I said, "let's live in the moment and not worry about the future."

Ethan pushed a piece of my hair behind my ear. "That's a big step for you. Are you sure?"

"No," I said, melting into his side. "But with you I don't need to know anything about the future except that I have your love and loyalty."

"Those are two things you have for as long as you desire."

"Oh, I desire much more than that," I purred, kissing him languidly.

"Good, 'cause I'm gonna give you everything you want and a whole lot more."

He flipped me over, pinning me to the floor, and I giggled like a kid. "Now where are those handcuffs?"

# Chapter 34

## *Eva*

*One year later*

I was standing in the middle of Ethan's living room—technically my living room as of two months ago—dressed in black biker shorts, a sports bra, and a neon-pink cropped tank. My hair was in a high ponytail, and I had a pink sweatband on my head. It was all a costume.

Ethan and I had cycled through most of the cliched role-playing characters—doctor/nurse, professor/student, cheerleader/football star, delivery man/homeowner, secretary/boss— switching who played which role to mix things up. And of course, we threw our favorite—Benson/perp —into the mix.

Today, he was the personal trainer, and I was the

client. I thought it would be safe for the surprise I had planned for him.

I tugged at the high waistband and shifted on my tennis shoe-clad feet. My stomach had disappeared, and in its place was my hollowed-out jumble of nerves.

Maybe it was a bad idea to do this. It was already a huge step that I'd moved in with him.

Since my grand gesture, the bubble of love had grown bigger to the point I was terrified it would pop. Nothing this fucking amazing could last forever.

After the devastation of my short-lived marriage, I'd been super cautious about leapfrogging too fast into this one.

Ethan wanted me to move in immediately. If he'd had his way, we would've been married and popping out kids the day after I told him I loved him. I was the one who said I wanted to take it a day at a time and not plan anything too far into the future.

Ethan thought I'd been body-snatched, but I assured him that for the first time in my life, I felt safe enough that I didn't need to map out every little step.

Despite all the men that had shit on me and deceived me and left—emotionally or physically—Ethan was different. He didn't leave. It hadn't been sunshine and roses every day, but he didn't run when it got hard, and God, I loved the way he loved me. He treated me like I was a drug and he was the addict. It was a major, grade-A turn-on for my sex and my heart.

Giggling came from behind the closed door of the walk-in pantry in the kitchen. Had it been a mistake to invite an audience for grand gesture number two? Rachel convinced me I'd want people here when I asked Ethan the big question. Which should be happening at any moment. I think she just wanted a front-row seat.

I pulled up the Excel file on my phone and double-checked it. Everything was ready.

I hadn't let go of all my organizational skills. Spreadsheets were practical, and it was still how I ran my day-to-day life...just not my relationship.

But today was different. As sure as I was that Ethan was head over fucking heels in love with me, I was trembling in my spandex.

I'd put training wheels on our relationship for the past year, but I was done with that.

On the distressed wood coffee table in front of me were several exercise bands, light weights, a yoga strap, and a narrow box that would fit a stack of papers but only had a single sheet inside it.

A loud chime rang out, indicating Ethan was in the elevator. I'd made him add this feature to his security system because I hated having no warning when one of us got home. The apartment would be empty and suddenly Ethan would appear in the kitchen or bedroom, and I'd scream.

Something crashed to the floor in the pantry.

"Hush," I hissed at the closed door, bouncing on my toes, unable to contain my nerves. "He's coming."

There was murmuring and shuffling and then quiet.

I nearly fainted when I heard Ethan's hard footfalls coming through the foyer.

"Ms. Hart?" he called out, and I smiled, a surge of giddy excitement attacking my organs.

"In here."

Oh God. Ethan looked ridiculous and panty-dropping hot all at once. His workout outfit was a spandex onesie like wrestlers wear. The shorts were so tiny his balls were practically hanging out.

It left very little to the imagination. My gaze snagged on the carved muscles of his legs and the thick mound between his thighs.

I bit my lip to hold back a moan.

"Good morning, ma'am." Ethan rounded me and slid his hands up my legs, stopping short of my ass. My sex quivered. "Very nice muscle definition."

I opened my mouth, but only a squeak came out. It was near impossible to concentrate when he touched me. Even after a year, I still became a wet noodle when he turned a heated gaze my way.

"We're going to start with some stretching. Get on your hands and knees." He pushed me to the yoga mat. I'd laid out on the rug, and I sank to all fours. Ethan leaned over me, his crotch pressing into my backside. Oh shit. He was already stiff.

"Ethan, wait," I said.

He ground the length of his erect cock between my ass crack, which he could do because we were both in spandex that left almost no barrier between us. Despite the four people hiding in the pantry, the material between my sex was soaked.

"No." I crawled forward, but he followed, gripping my hips to him.

"Ms. Hart, we haven't completed your session. I want you dripping with sweat when I'm done with you."

There was a muffled laugh from the direction of the kitchen, but Ethan was too distracted to notice. His hand circled my waist, but I flattened against the mat and rolled so I was several feet away. Another trick I'd learned in my self-defense classes.

"You have to stop," I said, panting. God, I wanted those people gone so I could ravish this man, but if I let him distract me, I may never go through with my plan.

Ethan tilted his head, a mischievous glint in his eyes, and I giggled. I fucking giggled. This gorgeous human undid me.

How did I ever think what I felt for Joe was love? It was nothing compared to the punch-in-the gut, fly-me-to-the-fucking-moon,  I-want-you-in-my-bed-my-pants-and my-heart-forever kind of love I had for Ethan.

And if he didn't agree to my proposal, I would die twice. Once from the embarrassment of having his sister, her kids, and Rachel witness my rejection and second because now that I knew what mind-blowing, never-want-you-out-of-my-damn-sight,  gonna-ravish-you-forever love was, I'd be a useless shell without it. Without Ethan.

Undeterred, Ethan scooped up the strap from the

coffee table and ambled toward me. He still thought this was part of the game.

An ear-splitting wail came from the pantry. Ethan's head shot up just as the pantry door flew open and Rachel, Savi, and both her kids burst out.

"What the hell?" Ethan flung me in front of him, hiding his massive hard-on from the crowd forming in the living area.

Beau squirmed in Savi's arms, crying to get down. He'd just started walking and didn't like to be contained now that he could move. Brynn burst from behind her mom and hugged me tight.

"Auntie Eva, are you married now?"

I hugged her little head against my hip, making sure to keep Ethan securely behind me.

"No, sweetie."

"What the hel—heck is happening?" Ethan scooted sideways, grabbed a pillow from the sectional, and held it in front of him.

"I'm sorry, babe," I said, unable to contain my laugh. "This was not how it was supposed to go."

Ethan raked his gaze over the little group of our friends and family. I'd debated inviting our parents, but it wouldn't have been complete without Joe's parents being there too. They'd been more of a family to Ethan than his own parents.

Joe and Ethan were still estranged, but Tiffany and Luis had made it clear that their son's disappointing behavior would not interfere with their relationship with Ethan. They came down once a month and had dinner with us. It was awkward AF at first, but if we didn't talk about Joe, it was good.

After our divorce, Joe had to move in with his parents, and Ashley swiftly dumped him and moved to Miami. Joe kept his word and paid all expenses from our divorce. I got the distinct feeling Tiffany and Luis made sure of this.

Even if he hadn't, I was never going to do anything with the videos I had saved. I'm not a monster. I'd been bluffing, and thank God it worked.

"The box isn't opened?" Rachel noted, picking it up from the table.

"Everyone. Shut up," I said, overwhelmed and needing to get through this.

Brynn clapped her hand over her mouth.

"Auntie Eva, you said a bad word," she said through her fingers.

"I'm sorry, sweetie." I smiled.

Savi, Brynn, and Beau were one of the best surprises to come from this past year.

Ethan and I often hosted the kids to give Savi a break. We always encouraged her to go out and get some, but she said all she wanted to do was sit in her house with no one touching her. The kids were adorable, and their unabashed love made my heart runneth over.

But I was glad to give them back by the end of the weekend. They were a shit ton of work. Totally worth it...in small bites.

Rachel opened the box and held it out to me. My

hands rested over my belly, protecting the big, scary fear of impending rejection from pressing up and out of my throat.

Ethan loved me. I knew it, so why was I falling apart?

"Come here, baby." He opened his arms, sensing my fear, and I stepped into them, soaking up his comfort.

"I love you," he whispered in my ear so only I could hear. "Now let's do whatever this is so I can take you into our bedroom and do push-ups over your pussy."

I choked out a laugh over a moan.

"Ethan said everyone has to leave immediately after this," I announced.

"Duh," Rachel said.

I sucked down a fortifying breath and took a small step back, Ethan's hands dropping to my hips, still holding on to me.

"Ethan," I began and took another deep breath. I needed to say this quickly and pray he didn't laugh. "There's no one in my life who's more important to me than you."

"Hey!" Rachel said in mock outrage.

I laughed and continued, Ethan's thumb rubbing the strip of exposed skin above my leggings. My racing pulse calmed as I stared into his sea-blue eyes.

"I used to lead my life from a place of fear, but because of you, I live it from a place of unapologetic love. You fell in love with me when I was in my darkest, Cruella-crazed frenzy, which is kind of a worry."

Ethan laughed, and I relaxed a little more. "And you calmed my crazy into a much more normal, fun place. I love playing with you. You keep me light and happy and safe. I didn't understand what it meant to be unconditionally loved until you, and I don't ever want to have to go out and find someone who would only ever be half as good as you. I thought a lot about everything I needed from you for this relationship to be my last relationship, and when I had every single thing sorted, I wrote it down."

I took the paper from Rachel and held it against my heart, my hands trembling.

"If you can give all this to me, then that's all I'll ever need. I don't need a ring, a wedding, kids, the money. I only want you."

Ethan slid the paper from my fingers but didn't look at it.

"Oh my God, will you two please get this over with." Rachel rolled her eyes. "I'm starving."

"I have to agree to everything on this list?" Ethan asked, his gaze locked on mine.

I nodded, my heart batting against my ribs so hard I nearly passed out.

"I don't have to look at it to know I'll give you everything on this paper and more," Ethan said. "I knew I loved you the moment I flung that silly corset thing off you."

I bit my lips together, holding back a waterfall of tears, and nodded to the paper. "Read it."

Ethan flipped the page over and read. Immediately,

tears filled his eyes. He choked out a joyful laugh, and in that moment, I knew he was mine.

"Forever," he read from the page. One word. That's all I needed from Ethan.

He crumpled the paper and wrapped me in a vise grip, kissing me, his lips pressing hard into mine, as if he was trying to express in this one kiss all the love he felt for me.

I got it.

The dizzying love I felt for him penetrated every fiber of me, flowing into every crevice of my being as he kissed me.

"Ew," Brynn's little voice whined from beside us.

"Get used to it," Ethan laughed, kissing me lightly one more time. "Because you're gonna be seeing Auntie Eva and me kiss until we're the ones wearing diapers, little lady."

"Grown-ups wear diapers?" Brynn asked, her face crumpling in disgust.

"Thanks for that, E." Savi gently tugged Brynn aside.

Ethan pulled me into his arms, and I gazed up at him, lost in his beautiful face.

"Is that a yes?" I asked.

He lifted me until my feet hovered off the floor.

"Hell yeah, it's a fucking yes."

"Well shit," Brynn said. "He said a bad word, too."

Ethan and I laughed into each other's mouths, then he took my hand, and we all went into the kitchen where champagne and juice boxes were chilling. My cheeks hurt from smiling, and I knew I meant what I'd written on that paper.

All I needed on my big, bad goal list was *forever* with Ethan Steele.

And I got it.

\* \* \*

\* \* \*

*When Rachel needs help, she turns to her grumpy new boss and ex-detective, Derrick to keep her safe. Hijinx and swoon-worthy mishaps ensue as they discover the surprising truth together.*

Get early access to *this close-proximity, age-gap raunch-com right now.*

\* \* \*

*She's a bedroom novice. He's stuck on his ex. But when he becomes her sexual instructor, sparks start to fly.* Read *Unbossly Manners* the first book in the Madly Bad at Love Series, right now.

*The Revenge Pact*

\* \* \*

*Catie's made a career out of lies. Sam's a sportswriter with a bad boy reputation. When she convinces him to start a fake relationship to save her career, his fire is (almost) too hot for her icy veneer!*
Dive into the steamy raunch-com FAUXMANCE IN THE CITY and get hot and bothered.

\* \* \*

# THANK YOU

If you loved Ethan and Eva's story, let other book lovers know by leaving a review at your favorite retailer. It doesn't have to be long. Just a sentence or two would be awesome.

# To My Awesome Readers

The start of the book was inspired by the awesome song "I Write Sins Not Tragedies" by Panic! At the Disco. The song starts with the groom lamenting about how he overheard a bridesmaid at his wedding telling a waiter that the bride was a whore. I thought... *wouldn't that make an interesting start to a story*. A rule in romance is to never write about cheating, but I was never one to follow the rules.

The building Ethan lives in is a real historic building on the corner of Spring and Elizabeth. I use to live across from it, back when it was a dilapidated rundown building that artists squatted in. Before the new developers began restoring it, they held an art show for all the artists in the building and lit candles in the windows. It was pretty cool.

Eva's phone being stolen was based on a true event that happened to my friend and me on the subway. Our dumbasses chased the kid that took my friend's phone out of the subway and through the streets of Washington Heights. He ran off, but we called the police and they used Find My Phone and caught the kid.

Please don't be like us. We were lucky. If someone steals your phone, be like Elsa...let it go.

Thank you to the early readers from my newsletter who fell in love with Eva and Ethan alongside me as I dripped the story out a chapter at a time. It was awesome writing this story alongside you all!

To my brilliant editors, Deborah Dove and Judy Zweifel. Your enthusiastic support, praise, and hard truths made this book shine.

To Elizabeth Mackey, my amazing cover designer. You nailed it!

To my Tuesday night writer's club. Thank you for all the support, wisdom, and margaritas. Writing can be a lonely affair but with all of you, I have found my tribe.

Thank you to my family (Mick, Skye, and Fia) for putting up with the mess that is me as I worked to get this story out. Skye, you've become a voracious reader (yes!) and one day, when you're older, I hope you don't cringe too much at all of Mommy's smutty love stories ;)

And finally, to all my readers. Thank you for your continued support and gracious emails and comments asking for more of my wacky and wild love stories.

xo
B

# Also by Brooke Stanton

## **The Love Charades Series**

*Fauxmance in the City*

She made a career out of lies. He's a sportswriter with a reputation. Can they fake it till they make it into each other's arms?

*Paradise Lust*

She's secretly in love with him. His ex wants him back. Will he see what's right in front of him before it's too late?

Coming Soon

*Love Bomb*

Coming Soon

## **The Madly Bad at Love Series**

(Sexy Romantic Comedies)

*Unbossly Manners*

*She's a bedroom novice. He's stuck on his ex-wife. But when he becomes her instructor, will sparks start to fly?*

*The Revenge Pact*

When Eva discovers her man is cheating on her, it's time for war. Her mission: revenge. Her secret weapon: the lying bastard's grumpy best friend.

Book #3

*When Rachel needs help, she turns to her grumpy new boss and ex-detective, Derrick to keep her safe. Hijinx and swoon-worthy mishaps ensue as they discover the surprising truth together.*

Get early access to this close-proximity, age-gap raunch-com right now.

## <u>The Forbidden Romance Series</u>

(In Kindle Unlimited)

*Breaking Josephine*

He needed a man to work his farm. What he got was her—a spitfire from Manhattan. Will their fiery tempers burn them to ash or ignite their love?

## Ruby's Passion

Moments after Ruby says I do, a secret rips her marriage apart. James is haunted by his bride's discovery. Can their hearts be mended, or is all hope lost?

## Lucy's Awakening

She married him to save her family. He married her out of duty. What happens when she breaks the rules and falls in love?

## Saving Kimi

Two men want her heart. She wants freedom. Is it possible to accept love, without losing it all?

## Serena's Silence

A tragedy took her voice. He's heartbroken and damaged. Can his wounds be healed in time to break her silence?

## Amy's Salvation

Her marriage is a sham. He's a brooding widower. Can they find love in an impossible situation?

## Margaret's Rapture

She's young and jilted. He's a bitter country doctor. When they're forced together, their fiery hate turns to a fiery passion that they're helpless to resist.

*Steamy Historical Western Romance Boxset*

Grab books 1-3 in the Forbidden Romance Series includes a bonus book and fun historical facts for each book.

# About the Author

In my early twenties, I moved to the single-gals playground—Manhattan—because my sister lived there and I could crash on her couch for free. Six years later (after a quick jaunt in London), I moved to Los Angeles, where I wrote a lifestyle column for an online magazine and lived a carefree life on the beach with my new hubby.

When we struggled with pregnancy, I did what I always do, I turned to writing and humor and created *Vagina Vacancy*, a blog about the highs and lows of IVF. It was a success—and I have two (mostly) sweet girls.

Creative writing was always my happy place, but it wasn't until I acquired an NYC lit agent that I realized writing could be a career. Unfortunately, the agent had to step away from publishing for personal reasons and I was left in a quandary. I had a manuscript I loved, but no one to sell it for me. That's when I joined my local RWA (Romance Writer's of America) chapter and entered my manuscript into their contest. To my delight, the book (The Misadventures of Catie Bloom) received second place.

That was 2015 when indie publishing was on the rise, and my fellow romance authors told me—when done right—it could be fun and lucrative. I'm a quick writer and business-minded and it felt like something I could kick ass at. So I took my award-winning manuscript, hired an editor from one of the top publishing houses, and I went to work.

The first book was a bestseller (woot!) and six years later, I've written and published three series, nine books, won multiple awards, and had numerous best-sellers.

And I fucking love it.

*Stalk me here:*
<u>brookestantonbooks.com</u>